DARIN

THE PRIDE OF THE DOUBLE DEUCE BOOK 4

KATHI S. BARTON

This is a work of fiction. Names, characters, places, and incidents are products of the author's imagination or are used fictitiously and are not to be construed as real. Any resemblance to actual events, locations, organizations, or persons, living or dead, is entirely coincidental.

World Castle Publishing, LLC
Pensacola, Florida
Copyright © Kathi S. Barton 2016
Paperback ISBN: 9781629893860
eBook ISBN: 9781629893877
First Edition World Castle Publishing, LLC, April 18, 2016
http://www.worldcastlepublishing.com

Licensing Notes

Cover: Karen Fuller
Editor: Eric Johnston
Editor: Maxine Bringenberg

CHAPTER 1

"Nope and double nope. I'm not going to do that for you, and I'm even more surprised, or pissed off you might say, that you even asked me to. Where do you get off asking me to...? I do not kill animals because someone is tired of them. Nor do I know anyone that might if I don't. Christ man, what if that were a child?" Mercedes went to the door and opened it for the man and his dog. "Get out. And if anything happens to that dog, and I do mean anything, I'm going to have you brought up on charges."

"For a dog? Fuck woman, it's a dumb animal. Nobody gives a shit if they get hit by a car. And if you think I give one shit about what kind of charges you think you can put on me, then you're way stupider than I thought you were." He jerked the dog along behind him as he made his way to the counter. With a short nod, Mercedes knew that her receptionist would take care of the man. And the dog.

Closing the door behind the two of them, Mercedes sat down on her chair and closed her eyes. This had been one hell of a week and it was only Tuesday. When her phone rang, she didn't even bother moving to answer it. She knew that someone would pick it up. As she sat there, Mercedes thought of her life so far.

She was a nearly thirty divorced mother of a ten-year-old little girl. No house, no car, and she was still paying off her ex-husband's debt like she'd had a thing to do with it. When she'd gotten her divorce from him he'd put a great many credit cards in her name and maxed them out. Nash hadn't been too happy that she'd been upset about him beating her to shit all the time. Go figure.

While she had a good job, there was little in the way of income that was free and clear for her, and she doubted even if she lived to be ten thousand that she'd ever see that day. She didn't have a car, no money for extras like socks or a thick winter coat, and some months she didn't even have enough food for both her and her daughter to eat.

When a knock at the door startled her to sit up, she nearly begged to be left alone. The bundle that came in the open door made her feel like she was queen of the world. Seeing Bonnie changed her mood just like that.

Bonnie was her life, and the fact that her father had had to give up all parental rights to her was the best thing that had ever happened to either of them. Holding Bonnie in her arms as she told her about her day, Mercedes wondered what the hell had happened to her to land her in such a state?

"You're not listening to me." Mercedes told her that she'd had a day and a half. "You work too hard. When do we get to go on that vacation? Soon, right? Can we leave tomorrow instead of Friday? I don't have any homework to turn in because of it being nearly Thanksgiving and all."

"It's not a vacation, but a job interview. I told you that." Bonnie nodded and handed her the things from her backpack. "This farm that we're going to, it might not be anything that we want. Or something might go wrong and I'm not good enough for them."

"Never going to happen. You're the best." Mercedes wished she had half the confidence in herself as her daughter did. "I've got my things all ready to go. And I even washed up your jeans for you so you could pack. I just have to put them in the dryer when we get home."

"Our ride isn't to arrive until Friday morning. So no, I don't think we can leave earlier. Besides, we have to close up the apartment before we go, and since I'm working late tonight, we'll have our work cut out for us tomorrow as it is. You can wait the extra day."

There was a car coming for them. Mercedes wasn't really sure what that meant for their travel plans, but Palmer had assured her that they were a very nice family with a great many horses that would need her help. Mercedes wondered how she and Bonnie were going to survive a trip all the way across the United States in a car, but they'd endured a lot together and this would be just one more thing. And Bonnie thought it was going to be an adventure.

Milly, the receptionist, came to the door to tell her she had a phone call. After telling Bonnie to keep it down, she answered the phone. She was both surprised and nervous to hear Palmer on the line.

"Hello, darling. I do hope you're ready for this trip. I know that everyone here is excited to meet you. I've told them so many good things about your work ethic." She told him that she was. "Good. Good. The car will pick you and Bonnie up at nine on Friday. Then you'll be taken to my plane and brought here. I'm sure you'll love it as much as I do. And we've put you two up in the bed and breakfast. You'll be the only ones in it, and I'm sure you'll give us some feedback on that as well. It's new to the area. One of the families that you're going to be working for owns it."

"I thought we'd be driving." He said that would take too long. "I see. And when we get there, what if things don't work out? I mean, this is just an interview. I want to be able to come back if there is a problem."

Palmer was quiet for some time, and she wondered if he was going to tell her that there wasn't an interview any longer, but they were bringing her out anyway. When she said his name, he asked her to hang on a moment, as he had someone in his office.

"Are we going to fly out?" She told Bonnie that it looked like it. "I've never been on a plane before. Do you think they'll have movies and stuff?"

"You're taking your things with you so you can watch what you want anyway." The line clicked again, and she started to ask Palmer if everything was all right when a woman spoke.

"Yes, everything is perfect. Hi, I'm Susie Douglas. My husband and I own the Douglas Ranch. I think there's been a mistake." Mercedes felt her heart break, and she told her that she understood. "Now don't be getting your panties in a twist. I didn't mean to say that you're not going to come out, but I think we forgot to tell you that we've already hired you. Palmer said you were the best and, to be honest with you, we sure could use the help. While most of the horses aren't sick, some of them are breeding and it's been a little hard on us getting to them in time."

"How many horses are we talking?" Silence on the other end made her think that there was more than the dozen or so she'd thought were there. "Mrs. Douglas? How many do you need me to come and see to?"

"See to? Not that many, a couple of hundred I guess. Not that many are breeding, but we need to get them a clean bill of health so they can be sold, and that's been hard on Jimmy, the local vet, to do. He isn't all that nice to the ponies either, so that doesn't help. But there are quite a few of them that are sold, and we need someone to come out and say they're healthy before they leave." Mercedes asked her daughter to go see Milly as Mrs. Douglas talked about what they needed.

"I don't think this is going to work out." Mrs. Douglas asked her why not. "Because I won't sign off on a health questionnaire knowing that you're selling less than healthy animals. I might be down on my luck, but I won't lie to help you make money."

"Good." Mercedes frowned at the phone and started to ask her what she meant by that when she spoke again. "I didn't ask you to sign off on their health records, did I? Nope. What I said was, I needed the paperwork to say they were healthy. Now to you that might sound like the same thing, but I will tell you that I can tell when a horse is sick or not a hell of a lot faster than you'd ever be able to. And as for you being down on your luck, I understand that as well. But I have no intentions of selling off our good name for a few extra bucks."

"I'm sorry." The woman at the other end laughed. "I think we might have gotten off on the wrong foot here. I'm not sure what's going to happen there, but if you've changed your mind then I can—"

"You're coming. Now, if you want. As far as I'm concerned you're hired, and we'll put you to work tomorrow if you want to get on that plane tonight and get here. We're about done in here. And with the number of horses we have, you might want to quit anyway." Mercedes asked her again how many she had. "At any given time there are as many as four thousand horses here. Double that in cattle, and we're bringing in a few extra animals to help out with the children as well."

Ten thousand animals? What the hell were they running out there? A breeding ranch? But Mercedes remembered that Palmer had told her that they were running a racehorse ranch, where men who had more money than brains came to buy stock.

"I have a daughter, you know that, right? She's all I have in the world and I have to see to her needs first and foremost. We don't know anything about the area or schools. I have no transportation either. Then there is housing and where we can live. Are there doctors in the area that are trustworthy?" Mercedes was making herself notes. A big dollar sign made her pause enough to ask about her salary. "I have to make enough money to get us settled. We have bills and we've been trying to pay them off."

"Hang on a second." When she was put on hold again, she thought that the woman was going to tell her that she'd have to make due. But Mercedes had already determined that she needed to make more than she was here or there was no point in leaving to move them across the states. "Okay. My husband and I are coming to you. Tonight. I know that you have to work until around five and that you're probably getting ready to pack and shit, but we'll come out there and talk to you. Bring the contract you can have looked over too."

"I don't have an attorney, Mrs. Douglas. And I can't afford to find one to look over this contract. I'm trusting you won't screw me over, because Palmer said I can trust you." She laughed, and Mercedes wanted to tell her again that she didn't think this was a good idea.

"We'll be there around four-thirty. Someone is making us reservations at the hotel and we'll have dinner. Palmer said he'd come, too, just to break the ice." Mercedes told her fine, but she wasn't making any promises. "No worries. And my name is Susie. Mrs. Douglas is too formal. We'll see you in a bit."

After putting down the phone, she sat there for a few minutes. The woman was like a tornado, and Mercedes wondered what it would be like working for her. More than likely she'd be swept up in whatever she had going on. If she worked for her, Mercedes thought there would never be a dull moment.

~~~

Susie hated to fly. And even more she hated to meet with new people. But this woman, for all her problems, was going to come and work for them. Susie had no idea why it was so important to her, but she needed Mercedes there on the ranch to help out. Looking over at the family that had come with her, Susie wondered if this had been a bad idea. She decided this was the best way to scare the poor woman to death if she wasn't already afraid of them.

"You should see her little girl. That Bonnie is a sweetheart. And something of a gifted child. That's another reason that she's so far behind on things. Putting Bonnie in that private school is costing her big time." Susie only nodded at Palmer. There was more to it than that, but she was going to wait for Mercedes to tell them. Gerard had had someone look into the woman before she'd agreed to hire her. "She doesn't like the shortened form of her name, by the way. I'm not sure what that would be, but she won't answer to anything but Mercedes. I think her ex called her anything but her first name and made it sound like a curse rather than an endearment."

"He's not going to be happy with this. I have a feeling that he's sort of possessive of his ex-wife and tries to rule her regardless of the papers that say he can't." Gerard leaned back in the seat they were in as he continued. "The man has to be loving that Mercedes is getting him out of debt. And the fact that he can go by her place once in a while to let her know what a disappointment she was to him. The man is going to have to learn to live without his punching bag sooner or later."

"He's going to be no problem as far as we're concerned. And if he makes a nuisance of himself, we'll take care of him." Mason nodded as he handed them a file. "There are some things on our new vet that I want to make you all aware of. First and foremost, she's good. Damned good, as a matter of fact. Top of her class in college. No problems from any of her clients. And the firm that she works for thinks a great deal of her. But that could be because they run her into the ground for little to no extra help in the financial department. She wants to be partner and they know it, so they fuck her when they can."

Susie glanced at Gerard and when he nodded, Susie spoke quietly. "I want to also make you aware of the things going on in her personal life. Her ex-husband is hurting them more than just with him coming by her place and knocking her around a little. He's somehow gotten access to both her place she's staying and her bank accounts. I think that he has someone watching her for him when she's at home. And more and more lately, he dips into her money when he finds that she has more than he thinks she should. He has buddies at the bank. Also, he's hiding funding from her. He gave up all rights to his daughter, but he's not paying child support to her because he claims he has no money." Palmer asked her how she knew this. "I've seen her. Once. I traveled out there to have a little talk with her to try and feel her out, and I never got past the first touch of her. Her problems aren't going to go away soon."

They were aware of what she and Gerard could do. Not all of it but a great deal. Some of it was just too fucking scary to share. Like the fact that they could touch a person and then know the people that they'd had contact with, the ex-husband being one of people that Mercedes had been touched by that day. The man was going to be an issue whether she moved out where they were or not.

"Do you think he's going to be a problem then?" Susie nodded, and Mason leaned back on the seat again. "A police problem or a leap problem?"

"Both," Gerard told them as he continued with the information they'd gotten from her. "He's not going to be happy when he finds out that she's moving. He likes her under his thumb. And he does have her there. Mercedes is afraid that he'll take her daughter from her and that he'll hurt her. Not legally, but simply to take her because he knows that it'll hurt Mercedes. He doesn't want her either, but he likes having control over Mercedes. The only reason she was able to file for divorce was because he was in jail just long enough for her to get a judge to grant her one, and when he got out, he was fucking pissed."

"And the money that she owes, is it because of the divorce or something more?" Palmer didn't look like he needed anyone to answer him, and when he spoke again, she was sort of proud of him. "He tried to ruin her. Or has he?"

"Close to it. She lost her house, her car, and can't get a loan. When she told me that she couldn't afford an attorney to go over the contract we're taking her, she wasn't kidding. They have nothing. Less than nothing. Next month the school that her daughter goes to is going to tell her that they can no longer carry her. She knows this, but can't stand the thought of losing it for her little girl. It's not only a good school, but a safe place for her too."

"We'll bring her back with us." Susie nodded at Palmer. "If I have to pack her up myself, I'm bringing her back with me."

"We all will. But I think we're going to have to go at this slowly. Think of her like a skittish horse or cow. She's terrified to trust anyone anymore, and when this ex finds out she's flown the coop, he's not going to lay back and just let her go." Mason asked her what she meant. "He's a man used to getting his own way. He's Nash Crosby."

Palmer didn't have any idea who that was, but Susie knew that Mason did. And so did Ed. Ed Clarke was the one that had told her and Gerard about him when she'd asked him about the divorce papers that she'd had sent to her. Crosby wasn't just bad news, but he made her own father look sort of saintly.

"Nash is...how should I say this? He is a man who is used to getting his own way, but it's more than that. He's a thug. And the worst kind of one. When he was younger, there was speculation that he might have been involved in the car accident that took both his parents' lives and that of his sister. Six months after they were gone, his grandmother died in a house fire." Ed looked at his notes as he mopped his brow with his handkerchief. "Then about eleven years ago, he married Mercedes Fisher. Her family had some money, but not a great deal. Mercedes was in her last year of veterinary college and making a name for herself even then. By all accounts, Mercedes didn't care for the man, had on several occasions gone to the police about him. Then one day there was an article in the paper that they were to be wed. Six months later, Bonnie was born."

"You think he raped her, got her with child, and then forced her into marrying him? That might have worked some years ago, but not now." Mason looked at Palmer when he laughed nervously. "Please tell me that I'm wrong about this."

"You're not. And she might not have married him had her father not been ill at the time. His death happened a few months after they said their vows. We think he might have been hurting her father, and that might be the reason that he got her to say yes. I guess we won't know for sure until she tells us." Susie didn't even look at them as Mason continued. She knew, but it wasn't her story to tell.

"So we're here to bring her to safety, not hire her." Mason told Palmer that they were going to hire her, had already as far as he was concerned. "Then I don't understand. Why all this cloak and dagger stuff? I really like this woman, but why do we need to know about her personal life like this?"

"She's going to be living on one of the ranches and we don't want anyone hurt. We have to consider what sort of baggage she'll be bringing with her in the form of that ex of hers." Gerard continued as Palmer agreed with him. "And if she's not happy, the horses and the cattle will know it. We can't have her stressed out when the horses have enough of that on their own."

As they were landing, she sat next to Gerard again. Susie had only touched the woman once, but it was enough to bring her to tears over what she was going through. Not only was the woman in desperate need of a break, but she was on the verge of losing even her home if her ex had anything to do with it. Nash was going to be a problem for them all.

The hotel was nice, and she wished that Darin had been able to come with them. He'd been hitting all the B&B's

around the country to find out what he wanted in theirs. The construction was nearly finished on the building, and the decorators had already finished up on three of the floors. In about a month, less she thought, they'd have all the rooms ready and Darin would have Douglas House up and running.

The restaurant, too, was nearly complete, and the new chef had been thrilled to death to take over the lower level for his own. Susie was still trying to keep herself from freaking out every time a bill came in, and finally, Gerard had told her not to open them anymore. It was expensive to start from scratch, and he assured her that they would be fine.

The business was going much better than they'd ever hoped it would, too. They were selling horses almost faster than she could train them. Several ranches had made the trip to their ranch to not only buy, but to place an order for other horses as well. Their monthly income was by far more than most people made in a lifetime.

They had expenses too; huge straw and hay bills, vet bills in the five figures weekly. Grain and feed was being delivered daily, and they still had to supplement that with an extra truck once in a while. But she was doing something that she loved, and they were doing well with it.

As soon as they were settled in their room, she called Darin to let him know about the room, even sent him a few pictures. Calling the doctor to ask her where they could meet, Susie was surprised when the little girl answered the phone. After telling her who she was and why she was calling, Bonnie started to cry harder. The noise in the background had her reaching for the others as the little girl sobbed in the phone.

"My daddy is here now, and he said that we weren't going anywhere. I don't know how he figured it out, but he's really mad at us." Bonnie cried harder when something sounded like it broke behind her. "Can you please come here and get us? Hurry, please? I don't want him here."

"They're coming. Where are you? Can you see them?" She told her that her mommy had told her to hide. "Good girl. You stay on the phone with me, and my family will take care that he goes home. Then you're going to come here with us and we're going to go to my house. We have a lot of ponies, and they're excited about you coming out."

Susie thought it important to keep the child on the line. She was afraid, and so was Susie. When another crash sounded very close to the phone, Susie brought up the trip again.

"Mommy said that we're going to fly away if we can." Susie told her that would be wonderful. "And that I can see the cows and horses that she's gonna take care of. If you hire her."

"She's already hired." There was a scream and then a man yelling for the little girl. "Don't go to him, Bonnie. Your mommy won't like it if he takes you from her."

Bonnie screamed, and the line went dead. Before she could reach for Gerard and the others, Gerard said they were there, and for her to call the police. She picked up the phone again with shaking hands and dialed the number. They said that they were on their way and that someone had already called them.

"There's a little girl in the house. She's ten and terrified. I think someone is trying to hurt her." The dispatcher told her that they were on the way, and would be there soon. "I hope so."

Susie was just going to go to them when she heard from Mason. He used the phone to contact her, and that terrified her more than she could have thought. When he spoke, his voice was calm and even, but she knew that he was beyond pissed off.

"I'd like for you to meet us at the hospital. The bastard has...we're still trying to find the little girl, but the woman is beaten to shit." Susie said she was leaving now. "Have our things packed up by the staff, and everything taken to the airport. We're not hanging around to see if he comes back to finish the job."

"How bad is she?" Mason said that the medics were there now, but she was talking to them. "She's gonna be worried about the bill. Tell her that she's insured as of three days ago when we hired her. And have the bills sent to our house."

"I'll take care of it." She thanked Mason and asked to speak to Gerard. "He's talking with the police, honey. As soon as he's done...he's fine, but he got hurt too."

She felt her legs shake, then she had to sit down. As she slid to the floor, she felt his touch, Gerard's touch, and his love as it surrounded her. Susie knew that Mason was still speaking to her, but the only person she cared about right now was the one in her heart and head.

I'm fine. It's a good thing that he hit me. She asked him how. *Because he assaulted me, and even if our vet doesn't press charges, I'm going to. This way he'll be in jail still by the time we land at home.*

So you're telling me you took one for the team? He didn't say anything. *How badly are you hurt? And so you know, I'm going to do ten times worse when I see you.*

Only a black eye and maybe a broken nose. She growled low at him. *If you want, I'll let you beat me a little before I take you hard on the floor. After, of course, I eat you.*

I dislike you very much right now. He laughed. *Come here to me, Gerard. I need to see you for myself.*

I love you as well. When we're done here. Meet us at the plane. We're out of here. She felt his anger. Sharp enough that she could almost taste it. *We have her. She came out when her mom told her to. The little girl has been hurt too. I'm going to kill this bastard.*

CHAPTER 2

Darin wasn't sure, but he thought he was missing something. The conference room was set up. The bedrooms, two of them on this floor, were also finished and ready and the beds made. There was even local art work on the walls. But he was missing something and it bothered him. As he made his way through both of those rooms again and in to the kitchen, he thought that maybe he was just stressed. In two days he had his first out of town businessmen coming in for a stay.

"It looks good." He grinned at his aunt. "What are you going to do about staff? I'm assuming that you're going to have them on call here."

"Yes. We have some of the pack coming in to work for us. Paddy said that they're mostly younger people. All of them are working their way through college or starting a family." Aunt Georgie sat in one of the comfy chairs he'd purchased for the conference area. "I'm missing something. I have no idea what it might be, but I can feel it."

Aunt Georgie looked around the room much like he had. "I don't know what it would be. It looks really nice. Maybe you can have someone that goes to these sort of meetings come in and tell you. Too bad Palmer isn't here. He'd be able to tell you right away."

"Yes. He'd know." Just as he was going to suggest maybe he should ask Emma, she walked in from the elevator. "Hello, sweetheart. I was just thinking about you."

She was just beginning to show. The baby she and Mason were having would be coming along in about six months. Jace's wife, Holly, was due in a few weeks and looked every bit as cute as she did uncomfortable.

"I have to tell you, Darin, I love the way you have it set up so that only a person with a card can come to a certain floor. That will be so much easier on guests, too. To know that no one can come in and bother them when they're in a meeting." She kissed Aunt Georgie on the cheek and sat down. "What did you need from me? Oh, and you should get some shades on the windows. I think they'll leave a glare on the computers when someone is sitting here."

"That's it." He kissed her on the cheek and made a call down to the front desk. The shades had come in two weeks ago, and since the windows hadn't been cleaned then, he'd forgotten to have them put in. After asking some of the crew to come up with them and install them on each floor, he went to sit with his family.

"I was just telling Aunt Georgie here about the vet they're coming here with. Her little girl has a broken arm, and the mom has some lacerations on her face and neck. Had the men not gotten there when they did, there is no telling what her ex might have done to them." Darin asked what had set him off. "He found out from her place of business that she was leaving town. I'm not sure why they'd do something stupid like that, but I'm having it looked into. This guy has been hurting the two of them for years, I guess."

"Mason said that she hasn't got much. A two-room apartment that's not in the best of neighborhoods. I thought that vets made a lot of money." Emma said that they did. "So what is her deal then? Or is it the ex?"

"He's been taking her things. Getting into her bank account. And he's put a lot of credit in her name, thousands of dollars' worth without her knowledge, and now she's responsible for it. He pays no child support and he has spies everywhere, Palmer told me. I guess they tell him her every move. There is also something about the divorce and his not wanting it. He's mad that she divorced him when he was away. He's very possessive." Darin got up to let the builders in and made some tea for the three of them. When he sat down, he thought about the women in his life as he looked around.

"I can't imagine any of you taking that from a man. You'd have killed him the first time he'd drawn back to hit you." Emma said she would have no problem knocking him around for just thinking it. "But how could you hurt your own child? I mean, he broke her arm, you said. Who does that to a child in the first place? But of your own flesh and blood?"

"I don't know, but we're going to protect her and the little girl from now on. Oh, and before I forget to tell you, because she's hurt, they're going to go out to the Mitchell ranch for a few days. The little girl wants to see a pony and Susie promised her that she would." Darin had already been told this by Gerard earlier. "Do you think you'll be okay next week? I guess you'll be a full house in a couple of weeks."

"I have one coming in on Friday. I'm glad for it. I think it'll be like a trial run for us. It's Guy Rose." He laughed. "The restaurant is going to open for them, just the men that are coming in, and then a grand opening on Saturday night.

Truman Rogers, the cook, he's been fussing over the menu for a week and a half now. I mentioned to him that he should just serve them sandwiches, and I think he was ready to cry. The guy is seriously stressed out."

"I guess there is no set menu, right?" Darin nodded at Emma. "I mean for lunch he'll have the same sort of thing, but not dinners. That's kind of scary. What if someone doesn't care for whatever he's cooking that night?"

"It's not like that. There will be a beef entrée, as well as a pork and chicken or fish. Vegetables will be the same for all three, and there will be two starches to choose from. Breakfast will be an open buffet kind of thing, with eggs or omelets to order. On the weekends there will just be buffet things. Fresh fruit and cereal. Coffee and juices for those who want it." He went to the file he'd brought with him today. "Here you go. This is the menu that he has planned for us on Thursday night. Then on Friday he'll serve the same thing unless we all hate it. I don't think we will, but we might have suggestions. There will be twelve men and women, I guess, and most of them will be staying at the hotel down the street."

Emma looked over the menu and smiled at him. "You've done a great job, Darin. I'm very impressed. Jace said you were taking night classes too, so you can have a better understanding of running a place like this."

"I'm having fun. And Jessie Edwards, my assistant, has been a great deal of help too. He's done this before, ran a B&B, but he said he has no desire to come and take over. He only wants to be a part of this, not the boss." He didn't have to tell them that the man had served a prison term for embezzlement. Darin trusted him not to hurt the company. And so did Susie and Gerard. "As of right now, the Douglas House is ready to go."

As they made their way down to the lower levels, Darin showed them all the improvements they'd made in the last several days. There was a bar, but it was closed off to the public. He had wanted a place where the people staying there could have a nice, quiet drink and not be bothered by anyone. There was also the spa and gym that they'd only just put in.

"We didn't need much in the way of equipment right now. And if we need more, there is plenty of room to expand." He moved back the door that opened into a large space that they'd done nothing with so far. "No pool, which I think is going to be more of a blessing than a bad thing. These men and women might want to relax and such, but I don't think they'll think of this place as a holiday. It's just too expensive for that."

Everything was included in the staying price. There was a special price, however, for people coming to the meeting and not staying overnight. This included lunch and dinner served to them in the restaurant, the two bedrooms, as well as anything they might need for the conference rooms, and wipe off board, pens, and paper. Even drinks, should someone desire them, could be worked into the one price. Darin thought it was pricey, but then he was having enough trouble trying to wrap his mind around anyone wanting to stay here at all, much less pay to do so.

Darin made his way back to his house after the women left him. His truck didn't want to start, but finally turned over and he made to the ranch. He was still trying to get used to having such a huge fucking house, but he loved it here. The McBrides had made him an offer too good to turn down on the house, and he'd been moving in almost the same day. Landon had come to see him a few days after they'd returned from their cattle drive.

"We can't live there anymore." Landon had said that before, just in passing; that the house, like the land around it, held too many memories. And few of them all that pleasant. "There was just too much there that I don't think we can ignore. And I think we're just too old to try."

"I don't know if I can afford the place, but if you'd rent it to me, I'll make sure that it's safe and no one tries to mess with things." Landon nodded but only played with his drink. They'd met at the bar in the Douglas House while it was still under construction. "Landon, you can trust me not to do anything bad to your home."

"I know that, boy. I know that better than anyone." He nodded before continuing. "Katie and I talked about the house while we were gone. Just at odd times one of us would bring it up. We figured that was the best way to deal with what he'd done to us. Not grieve over what we lost, but to take it out and look it over a little at a time. Anyway, we talked and we decided that we want you to buy it off us. I'm making you a one-time offer for it."

"Landon, I'm a poor man. The only income I have coming in right now is barely enough to cover my rent and my cell phone bill. And I'm driving a truck almost as old as your daughter. As much as I'd like to buy the house from you, because it is a really nice house, I just don't have the funds for it. Much less a down—"

"You listen to me here. I said I have you an offer, and you'll let me tell you about it." Darin remembered thinking he was in deep trouble, but then he smiled at him. "A dollar. That's all we want for it, and the promise that you find you a mate and take as good a care of her as you can. Bring you up some babies in that house. Just like me and the missus did. And be happy."

"Landon, I don't think I can—"

He put his hand up and Darin had shut his mouth. "You know as well as I do that I don't have any use for any more money. Hell, I got more now than I could spend if I lived another hundred years. And that brother of yours is making us more every day with his new ideas. But to see some other yahoo living there would plum break my heart. I know you, son. I know your family. If anyone was going to be good for that house, I know that it will be a Douglas boy." He wiped at his face, tears streaming from his eyes. "He done hurt us, Dirk did. Not just with that bat when he took it to me, but in our hearts too. I know that we should have done something more about him, but I just.... If you'd do me this favor, Darin, live and love in that house, I know that someday I'll be able to forgive myself for the fact that I'm glad that my son is gone."

Not only had he gotten the house, but the contents too. The only thing he'd had to do when he moved in was to put his clothing in the dressers. The rest was finished. Darin was almost afraid of his good fortune.

~~~

Mercedes held Bonnie to her on the trip to Ohio. There were so many things going through her mind right now that she wasn't sure that she could single out one to concentrate on. When Susie sat beside her, Mercedes felt her face heat up. To have a potential boss see her looking like this was embarrassing.

"She's very brave, your little girl." Mercedes tried not to look at the pink cast on her daughter's arm. "When I was talking to her before the men arrived, she was so calm and quiet. And she knew to stay on the line until the others got there. She told me that you told her to hide. I'm sorry that you had to teach her that."

"He was there when we got home. Not in the apartment, but close enough that I wasn't able to get in and lock him out." Not that Mercedes thought that would have stopped him. "Someone at my work told him that Bonnie and I were going out of town on a job interview. It doesn't take much to set him off, and this was a big one."

"Why would they do that?" Mercedes had an idea but didn't voice it. "We've had you investigated, as I'm sure you know."

"Yes. I would expect no less of you. I'm sure that whatever you found, only about half of it is true. Nash has a way of getting people to do what he wants them to do, no matter how it hurts them or others." Susie asked her if she meant her office. "No. I think they were afraid I'd get the job and then they'd have no worker for when they wanted time off. I've been on call more than I've not in the last couple of years. I had hoped that it would pay off, but...."

"I don't blame you. Working there now would have been stressful since they're the ones that are responsible for you and Bonnie getting hurt." Mercedes looked at Bonnie again. "I wanted to answer some questions for you now. If you're up to it."

"You must think I'm a fool." Susie asked her why she'd think that. "I married this man because I had no choice. And before you say that everyone does, I really didn't. He abused me to the point where I was in the hospital more than I wasn't. The police were no help. Not even when I put out a restraining order on his ass. When he started to get into my bank account, I would only put enough in there to satisfy him but kept the rest for the two of us. How stupid is that? To hide money from the very man who fathered my child." Susie said nothing for several minutes. "Why are you hiring me? Really?"

"Palmer knows you to be a good vet, as well as a good person. He talks on and on about your little girl as well. There are others too, that said glowing things about you. Most of them have never worked with you, but in the type of business that we're in, word gets around faster than a flu at a grade school." Mercedes didn't get the chance to ask her who as she moved onward. "My husband and I run a ranch with more ponies on it than most people seen in all their lifetime. We also graze cattle and steer on the same land. There will be some donkeys as well as a few goats that you might have to see to if they get ill. There are cats too, small barn cats that keep the children that come out entertained. The pond in the back of the property has ducks on it most of the time. Deer, as well as a whole lot of other animals, run the woods. You'll be very busy when you're ready to start working."

"And you want me to care for them all? That's a lot for one person to take on, even if I do have glowing reports." Susie nodded and smiled at her. "I'm not going to be alone in all this, am I?"

"No. But I do need to make you aware of a few things. You're going to hear and see things that you might not understand. I just want you to keep an open mind about whatever you might hear or see and ask questions before you run off in the night. And you're also going to think me and my husband mad, but we're not. We both have a gift." Susie put her finger on her daughter's arm. "Bonnie is at the top of her class right now. They have a spring fling coming up that she's glad that she's not going to be going to. Her classmates make fun of her because she's poor. Not that she's told them, but she thinks they just know because they're mean. Her teacher doesn't care for her, or so Bonnie thinks. There is a little boy in her class that teases her terribly about the backpack that she carries. She's terrified that you're not going to like it at the ranch and she'll not get to ride a horse. There is more that I can tell you, but for now that should be enough. Would you like for me to touch you?"

"Who told you that?" Susie shrugged, and Mercedes pulled her daughter closer to her. "You've been spying on us? Is that how you're going to make me work for you? You think to blackmail me or something and that I'll do as you want?"

"No. I know this is going to sound strange, but I can feel everything there is to know about you. And not only you and other humans, but animals as well. I can't actually talk to them, but I can communicate with them. It's how I can know when they're in pain a great deal better and faster than you can." Mercedes started to shake her head. "I can. And so can my husband."

"What are you?" The question made all the others look at her. And had they not been on a plane high in the sky, Mercedes would have gathered her daughter up and left them. "You're not human."

"No, we're not." Mercedes started to shake her head and stand when Susie touched her arm. "You have to listen to me, Mercedes. I know things about your ex that might just save you and your daughter's life."

Mercedes sat down but away from Susie. "I don't understand what's going on here. You're scaring me and I don't like it."

"He's hired a man to watch over you. The man in the apartment across from you and Bonnie. His name is Jacks." Mercedes nodded. "Several weeks ago, he was to get into your house when you weren't looking and take your house key and make a copy of it. He did this. Your ex-husband had cameras set up around the place to keep tabs on you. He watches you sleep and shower too."

"No. I don't believe you." But she did. There had been times when she knew that someone had been in her place. Sitting on her bed, touching her things. "Why is he doing this to us? We're not his to rule anymore."

"He does it because you got the divorce and he wasn't able to stop you. And now that you have left, he's going to make it so that you never leave him again. There are people coming for you. He's one of them, but they're coming and they won't stop until he gets what he wants." She looked at Bonnie, then at Susie again. "You know that I'm not lying to you. You know what sort of person he is."

"He told me when we were married that I'd be his until I was dead. He married me, forced me into it, or he'd have killed my father." Susie said nothing, but Mercedes had a feeling that she knew. The woman was either too clever or she was what she said she was, someone who could read her memories. "Is he safe?"

"Yes, your dad is safe. No one knows where he is but you, Gerard, and I. As soon as we get home I'm going to have a few men go get him and bring him to live on the ranch with you and Bonnie. I want you to know right now that nothing will happen to you so long as you believe in us and that you do as we tell you. Your father, he's going to be safe as well." Mercedes looked away. "I'm very sorry to have done this to you like this. But you have to know that there wasn't any time to sugar coat things."

"When Nash finds us, he'll kill us all." Susie told her that he'd try. "You don't know him like I do. When we were married, he had a gun to my head and a man standing near us with one pointed to my father's head. The clergy acted like it wasn't that big of a deal. I don't even know why he wanted to marry me."

"Because you said no." Mercedes just sat there thinking of the conversation that she'd never been able to have before. Not with any of her friends, and especially not her daughter. "There's more I'd like to tell you, but I think you've had enough for now."

"Yes. More than enough I think." Susie said nothing more but didn't move away either. "I have to find somewhere that's safe for us. My daughter will need to go to a school that won't allow him to take her when he wants. My father…if you know about him, then you also know that he needs special care."

"The school that we have set up for her is going to be safer than any you can think of. By the time that your father is here, the ramps for his wheelchair will be done and the bathrooms renovated for him." Mercedes felt like a heavy stone had been put on her shoulders. "You'll be as safe as you let us make you. I promise you that."

"Yes, but I've been promised things before and it never seems to work out for me." Susie said nothing. "I'm really tired. Can you tell me how much longer we'll be?"

The pilot took that moment to announce that they were ten minutes from landing. Waking Bonnie enough to get her buckled in, Mercedes felt like she was on one of the rides that went in circles, round and round until your skin was pulled back. She wondered if anything would ever be normal for her again.

CHAPTER 3

Darin showed the man how to work the elevator, then stood back while he made his way up to his room. The man with Mr. Rose, Scott—Darin's new-hire—was only seventeen and terrified he was going to fuck things up for himself, but Darin wasn't worried. All he had to do was take the luggage up to the bedroom and lay it out. Then ask Mr. Rose, a horse buyer from Kentucky, what he needed in the way of supplies. Darin made his way back to the desk to see how things had gone there.

It had thrown them a little when he'd shown up a day early. Things were ready with his rooms, but the dining area had been booked for their family and not available to use. Darin thought, all in all, they'd done well with the unexpected guest. He asked Jessie if there had been any problems.

"No, everything went well. He paid for the weekend and told me that he had ten more coming in Saturday morning. I've arranged for several cars to go and pick them up at the airport and have refreshments in the cars when they do." Darin told Jessie that was a great idea. "Since they're arriving at around two, I'll have Truman make them some light snacks and a fruit tray to tide them over until dinner that night. Mr. Rose is early, as you know, so he said that he'd take care of his own dinner tonight. You never said if they were human or not."

"I don't know, to be honest. How would we even find that out?" Jessie was a bear and didn't care all that much for green leafy, nor did he care overly much for anything healthy. Jessie said that he had no idea. "I guess we'll have to play that by ear."

"Also, I think in the future we should put bottled water in the fridges. Pitchers and glasses could be expensive if broken. Also, carting ice up every hour or so could be distracting. Then we can have a recycling bin put out to show that we're green." Darin nodded, already thinking of where to put it. "Since we have the kitchens laid out the way that we do, I was also thinking that we could store plates, the ones that we use for the rooms, somewhere in them."

"I've already taken care of that. In the bottom counter next to the sink there are a hundred plates, napkins, as well as silverware. We might not use it all per stay, but we can at least have it there in the event that we do. That way when we bring in their buffet during meetings, it'll be one less thing we have to cart up there." Jessie marked that off his list, along with the other items he'd mentioned. "My family is coming into town soon. Don't forget that we're having dinner in the restaurant as a trial run for Truman. I think he'll be fine, but he wants this."

"Very good." Jessie started away but turned back to him at the last minute. "Your aunt called. She said to remind you to tell Truman that there would be two more for dinner. The young vet, as well as her daughter."

Darin made his way to the kitchen to let Truman know, completely forgetting that she'd told him last night. Truman was standing next to the stove, just staring at it, when Darin said his name. Truman looked at him with a glazed look, and Darin felt his cat run along his skin.

"I'm not sure I can do this. I was...this is a big deal, and I'm going to fuck it up for you." Darin told him he was going to be fine. "No. I'm not. I have twelve people for dinner tonight and the chicken that I have planned is going to be trashed, as the buyer got a deal for a reason. It's bad. I can't seem to get anyone to make the side dishes right, two people quit before I got the pleasure of firing them, and I'm having a hard time thinking beyond the fact that I'm going to fail."

"Okay, first, there are going to be fourteen of us." Truman groaned. "It'll be fine. I'm calling in some help for you. Julie, the pack master's wife, has been begging me to let her come in and assist you. She has a couple of relatives, too, that want to come to play in a big kitchen. And trust me when I tell you, these women can help you in ways you won't even realize you need."

"So hire them." Darin told him to get a grip as he picked up the phone. Ten minutes later, not only did he have a crew coming in to help, but he also had called the buyer for the chicken, who refunded their money. "I still have no chicken."

"Ah, but you underestimate me. Not only do you have the money back in your coffers, but there are two dozen steaks coming to compensate you for his mess up." Truman started nodding, and Darin could almost see his mind working on a new menu. "Julie said she'd make dessert for you if you've not made it yet."

"Yes. Fine." Truman moved away from him, and Darin felt like he'd just averted a huge disaster. "Can I hire who I want?"

"It's your kitchen. That was our deal." Truman nodded again and stopped to look at him. "What now? Anything else?"

"I thank you for this. You gave me a chance when we both know that you shouldn't have." Darin said nothing but moved out of the kitchen. Yeah, well, little did Truman know that he'd given Darin a bigger one by saying that he'd work for him.

Most everyone that worked for him had a brush with the law at one time or another. Some of them had been painted up pretty good with the brush, but they were people that needed a hand up. Darin had wanted to do something for the people that he'd met in the kitchen Landon had set up for the homeless, and this was his way of doing what he could. Emma had helped him figure out background checks, Aunt Georgie had gone way above what he'd asked of her in finding shoes and uniforms for them, and even Mason had provided car service to and from the shelter for those who had no cars yet. Others rode bikes or simply walked, but it was working out for them all.

"Hey, Darin. We just got back from out west. I'll talk to you about it later." He moved toward Mason when he came in the front lobby. "I'd like for you to meet someone. This is Bonnie Crosby. Bonnie, this is my brother Darin. He owns this place."

When she put out her good hand to shake his, Darin took it and felt the nice firm grip. He thought he might like this kid. His one weakness was children, and blonde, blue-eyed little girls were the best. Smiling at her, he asked about her cast.

"My dad did it. He wasn't really happy that Mom and I were leaving to come here. He's not a nice man." Darin glanced at Mason, who shook his head. "He hurt my mom too. Beat her up pretty good."

"I'm really sorry about that. I hope the two of you are better now that you're here with us." She didn't say anything but looked at Mason. There was something there, some hero worship, Darin thought. "I was wondering if I could sign your cast for you. It's been a long time since I've been able to do that for any little girl. And I love the pink."

"Miss Susie said I should have any color I want. They didn't have any rainbows, but she said she'd work on that for me. She's really nice, and Mom likes her." Darin nodded and stood up. She backed from him, but he didn't let that bother him too much. If her dad did do this, then he could understand her fear. "You're very big, huh?"

"I am. But I do have something over here that might make you happy." He started walking away and was surprised when she walked alongside of him. As they made their way to the front desk, he told her what he was going to do. "I have some new markers back there that I've not used yet. And how about if we put a rainbow on this thing for you?" He had Jessie hand over the box of markers he'd been using to make charts.

"You can draw a rainbow? I'm okay with it, but this is my right arm and I can't use it." He wasn't sure the real order of the colors, but after telling her his problem, she smiled at him. "I'll help you. The first color at the bottom is violet."

Mason walked to where they were, Bonnie sitting on the chair behind the counter and him standing next to it. Mason leaned close and asked him for a favor.

"I was going to see if she can hang out with you for a little while. About an hour." He asked him what was going on as he opened the indigo marker. "Her grandda is arriving soon, and we want to get them settled in. He's going to be staying with us for a little while. At least until we can find a home for them."

"Sure. We can have some fun together, can't we, Bonnie?" She nodded as he put the next color on her cast. Blue had been applied, and so had green. Mason thanked him and told him he'd be back later. Darin was working his way up to yellow when she told him she was hungry. "I can take care of that too. Come on. We'll see what my friend Truman has to snack on. I forgot to eat lunch today."

Bonnie followed him to the dining area when they had the rainbow done. Darin thought it looked pretty bad, but Bonnie said it was perfect. He supposed that at some point in your life you forget the colors of a rainbow, and was glad that she'd reminded him of how pretty they were. When asked, Truman said that he'd fix them right up, and the two of them sat in the kitchen while he made them some lunch.

"My mommy is going to work for Miss Susie." Darin told her he knew that and that Susie was his brother's wife. "There sure are a lot of you guys, huh?"

"Yes. I suppose there are. My aunt raised us when my parents died." Truman set a plate of grilled cheeses in front of the two of them just as Julie and two of her sisters came in. After getting her set up with what she needed, Darin sat back down with the little girl. "You excited about starting school soon? That lady over there, Mrs. Luna, she's one of the teachers. I think she teaches fourth grade."

"I'm in fifth. I took some tests and they moved me up. I don't like it. The kids all make fun of me." He asked her why. "Because Mom and I, we don't have a lot of stuff. Sometimes when I don't have my fees right away, they call me names. And they hate my backpack."

"Your backpack? What is wrong with it?" She got down off the chair and moved out of the room. He wasn't worried about her, Darin knew there were plenty of people around to keep an eye on her. When she returned and handed it to him, he noticed that it was worn and tattered. He started to tell her that he'd get her a new one when she spoke first.

"It was my mom's when she was in college." Darin nodded and saw the pins that were holding the front zipper closed. "She said I could have a new one, every year she tells me that, but I love this one. It's special because even though she had to work three jobs and borrow tons of money, she did it. And I'm going to carry it until I go to college and pass this one on to my little girl."

Darin could see the love that was between mother and daughter in the way that Bonnie touched the safety pin that served as a zipper tab. There were other things on it too. A patch that had been handmade, as well as a couple that had been bought. He'd bet anything that they weren't just decorations, but were also covering some place on it that had broken through. When he set it on the table between them, he looked at Julia as she stood nearby. At her nod, he looked back at the little girl who had stolen his heart in only a few minutes and talked to her about coming out to the ranches.

~~~

Mercedes looked around the room her dad was in. He was happy, she could tell that. And not just with being there with them. When she'd gone with Mason and Emma to pick him up, he'd cried for twenty minutes about how much he'd missed her.

"You like it here, daughter?" Mercedes smiled and nodded. Her dad had called her daughter since she'd been a little girl. "And this job, it's going to keep you away from that bastard ex-husband of yours?"

"Yes. I hope so. Everyone says that they'll protect me, but we both know what sort of person he is." Her dad nodded and rolled his chair to the desk that had been brought in for him to use. "They said that the bathroom is ready for you to use too. Did you look at it?"

"I did. These people went to a lot of trouble to put up an old man they don't even know. I even heard that one of them has got them a nice sized van to cart my bottom around in. Been a long time since I've had me any pampering. You too, I'm betting." Mercedes had been told that too. "Why do you suppose they're going to such trouble for us? I don't mean to sound like you don't deserve it, but honey, they don't know me from shit."

"I keep asking, but they said that they need me here and that's why they're doing it. I have yet to go to the ranch, but I'm getting excited about it." He told her he was too and looked out the window that faced the lovely pool behind the house. "Mason said that there is a lift out there too. That Emma's grandma put it in when she broke her leg skiing once. This used to be her house, I guess."

"Emma told me that her grandmother was a pistol. I can see that if her granddaughter is anything like her." Mercedes nodded and sat on the bed. There was a lift on it as well, so that her dad could get in and out of the bed by himself if he wanted. "I'm to understand that there is this big dinner thing tonight that you're going to. Mason invited me too, but I don't think I'll go. It's a lot to travel when you have to be lifted up and down like they have to me. I'd just as soon go to bed early. Watch some television."

"You should go, Dad. Bonnie will be there with me, and this way you can meet the people who are taking care of us." He said he'd think on it. "Dad, I'm sorry about this. You know that, don't you?"

"Daughter, I know that that man hurt you, and that had you not hidden me away, he would have continued to hurt you by getting to me. But we're going to make it here, I just feel it in my poor old bones." She nodded. "I wish someone would put him out of his misery. It sure would make me sleep better at night just knowing that he's not going to be jumping out of some dark alley like he's been known to do."

"Me too, but I don't think we should wish for his death." Her dad told her that was the only way some people knew to quit. "Maybe so, but I don't think killing him is the only answer. Maybe a long prison term would suit him better."

"He'd be out someday. Dead is forever. And I'm thinking that he'd get to you even from behind bars. That man has a long arm and no sense of what's right." Mercedes got up and kissed her dad on the forehead before moving to the door. "You're gonna come back, aren't you? I mean today?"

"I live here too, Dad. I'll be back every night. I just have to go and figure out where my workplace is, as well as supplies I'm going to need for the office here. Susie said that they'd put one in at the horse ranch, too. I need to tell her what sort of things, drugs and such, I'm going to need to get started." He asked her to take some pictures. "Come on out with me. You can pretty much go and come as you please, Mason said."

"I don't want to be a bother." Mercedes could see that he really wanted to go. "You know they put in a ramp for me too? Right out there on the deck, like it was something that they'd meant to do all along."

"I'm sure that they expect you to use it too." She opened the door for him, and he rolled toward her. "We'll make our way to the offices first. Gerard said that they were near the barn."

There was a lot of construction going on today and lots of men and women working around the ranch. Several dozen of them were working on a big building that looked nearly completed. Mercedes wondered if that was the dairy that they'd been talking about. She knew that this family had money. While the men seemed to be a little less comfortable with their wealth, the women for the most part seemed to fit it like a well-worn rug. Not Susie. She was like her, or used to be. Poor as a church mouse, as her dad used to say.

The building she was using for a sort of clinic was right where Mason had told her it would be. But the size of it was breathtaking. The office building that she had worked at before would have fit in this one nicely, and this was all hers. And it was well equipped too. Her dad was looking over some of the cabinets and their contents when someone walked in the room with them. Mercedes moved to stand near her father.

"My name is Landon McBride. Emma is my little girl. I didn't mean to startle you, darlin'." She nodded but didn't move. "I heard tell you were a might skittish. That's all right, sweet pea. I'm sort of, too, around a pretty young woman. My wife said I'm harmless and I am."

Ignoring his flirting, Mercedes pointed to her dad and made the introductions. Mr. McBride moved toward him and shook his hand. The two of them seemed to hit it off really well, and Mercedes felt herself relax a little. There were so many new people coming and going here, she couldn't help but be nervous. Hearing a car pull up out in the drive, she looked out the window to see her daughter being let out.

Moving out to catch her, she was knocked over when she came running at her. Mercedes was still laughing when Mr. McBride gave her a hand up. It was so nice to have her daughter being this happy again that she didn't care at all to be dirty. Mercedes introduced her to Landon, as he'd asked to be called, then her father. Bonnie took to her dad like they'd been together all her life, but her dad was as emotional as she was.

Her father sobbed for ten minutes when he met his granddaughter for the first time. Mercedes decided right then if she could have this kind of happiness every day, she'd almost work for the Douglas McBride ranches for free.

While she made her list, keeping an eye on Bonnie and the men around the ranch, Mercedes decided that she was going to enjoy this as well. The equipment was new and up to date. There was enough room for her to take care of just about any animal that came to see her, and they'd even provided her with a car big enough for her entire family to get around in so she'd not be stuck at any one place. Susie came in to see her just as she was putting the last few things on the list.

"I'll take you over to the other station in the morning. But they have the same lay out with the same equipment. Mason pointed out that we didn't want you to have to wait on equipment or whatever if it was needed at one of the other ranches. But for now, we're about ready to go into town, and I know you don't want to miss that." Mercedes wasn't so sure and said as much to her. "It'll be fun. You'll see. And you'll meet the rest of the family. I know we can be a bit overwhelming, but getting it over with all at once will be better for you. And they promised to be on their best behavior. I wouldn't count on it, but they said they'd try. Really, there are only two more brothers to meet. I think you've met the rest of them."

"Yes, Zack and Darin, I think their names are." Susie nodded. "My daughter is quite taken with Darin. He drew a rainbow for her on her cast and took her to lunch. She said that she also got to be taste tester for some scones for tomorrow, as well as some sort of salad dressing. I'm surprised that she even consented to a salad. Normally, she's not a big fan of green and leafy."

"Neither are we, but we make an effort." Susie laughed as they made their way out of the building. "Mercedes, remember when I told you about seeing strange things around here? And that I wanted you to keep an open mind?"

"Yes." As soon as she saw the wolf, Mercedes froze. Her daughter was petting the biggest wolf that Mercedes had ever seen. "Is that your pet?"

"No. He's our neighbor and friend. I'm sorry to have to do this to you, but things are moving faster than we expected. The wolf is a shifter. His name is Paddy Sexton. His wife is Julia. They live in the house about four miles from here." Mercedes looked at her, then back at her little girl who was playing with a smaller version of the big wolf. "That's his son, Patrick. He'll go to school with Bonnie. They're shifters. Like we are."

"No." Susie nodded that they were. "No, I don't believe in shifters. I...they don't exist. They're made up, like in books."

"No, we're very real. I'm telling you this now because I wanted you not to be afraid when you come upon one of us out in the woods, and you will. We run here, that's why it's important that we have plenty of land. And we share with the other shifters around here too." Mercedes was still shaking her head. "We're cougars. All the Douglases are."

"But you're a person." Susie assured her that she was that, too, and put out her hand. As the dark fun started to grow over her arm, Susie started telling her about how she was born a cougar but the other women had been turned. "This isn't real. I don't know what's going on, but this isn't real."

"It is real. Paddy is a pure blood too. As is his wife." Mercedes backed away from her as she continued. "Your father knows what we are. He didn't know we were cougar's, but that we weren't human. He said that you'd be harder to convince. I want you to be okay with this."

"Dad? What is she talking about?" He nodded at her, and she sat down on the floor. "I don't understand this. Any of this."

"Honey, that's why they can protect you so well. They're not human, and when that bastard comes here, they're going to protect you like nobody else can." Her father took her hand in his. "Mercedes, look at them. They'd no more hurt you than I would."

"But I don't believe this." As the world started to narrow down to a pinpoint, she saw movement out of the corner of her eye and fell back when one of the men in the yard went from man to beast. A huge fucking cougar was standing beside the equally large wolf.

CHAPTER 4

Darin walked around the table again, just to be sure, he told himself, and smiled when he saw that everything was as perfect as it could be. He looked up when Truman came into the room with several baskets of breadsticks. Darin took half of them and helped place them on the table.

"I cannot thank you enough for bringing me help. Christ, Julia can work for me full-time if she wants to. And Candace Luna can come here and bake bread for us every day of the week if she wants. Hell, I'd even pay her out of my own pocket to have her do it." He pulled one of the still warm breadsticks out of the basket in his hand and handed it to him. "These are what she called last minute sticks. They took her less than two hours to put together. I have several dozen of them that are unbaked in the freezer now for the next few days."

As he munched on the wonderful bread, Darin asked him about the others. "I hired two of the high school kids to come in and wash up for us when we serve dinner. They're saving for a car. Also, there is a man coming in tomorrow to help me with the breakfast buffet set up. I've never done one of them before, putting it together, but I was assured that he's good at it."

"Bill. Yeah, he works at the homeless shelter. When the thing came in, the instructions were less than helpful, but he got it together in no time. He'll help out." Truman nodded as he put the flower vases on the square table that would hold all of them for dinner. "This is nice. I thought you'd have us at one long table."

"Julia. She said that if we boxed up the table like this, that you'd have more room to move your elbows, as well as everyone could talk to each other. Christ, Darin, you should have hired her instead of me." Darin said nothing as he picked up one of the name plates by the plate closest to him. "Bonnie made those for me when you were on the phone. I had to use them. She did me a solid when she said my dressing needed more mayo. That kid is wonderful."

He put the name plate down and smiled at the way she'd drawn a rainbow on each one of them. Darin had had a wonderful time with her this afternoon and had hated to see her leaving with Mason. As soon as Jessie told him that the first cars were arriving, he told Truman that it was going to be great and left him to it. Darin was standing at the desk when his aunt and Palmer came into the lobby. He was glad now that he'd pulled on a tie and jacket to have dinner. Everyone, it seemed, had dressed up too.

His aunt and Palmer had married two weeks ago. And Darin and the rest of his family had sent them on a short cruise from which they'd only just arrived back a few days ago. He was so happy for Aunt Georgie and Palmer and the fact that his aunt was living a wonderful life now. Darin wondered if Logan was going to take over the family homestead as he'd been threatening to do for a few days now.

Palmer hugged him tightly after Darin kissed Aunt Georgie on the cheek. "My boy, this is spectacular. Very open and inviting. A man would be a fool not to enjoy having his business meetings here." He told Palmer that he thought so as well. "I bet the rooms are just as lovely. Emma said that when she was here earlier that you'd gotten all the blinds hung."

"Yes. She just took one look around and knew what was missing." Darin invited them to go up and have a look around while he and Jessie waited on the rest of the family. He was still standing at the front desk when Bonnie came running toward him. "Hello, my dear. I hope you're enjoying your stay here with us so far. Emma said you have her old room from when she was a child there."

"It's all girly and stuff." He grinned at her. "I'd rather have one with horses and cowgirls, but Mom said that we have to be nice."

He wanted her to come out to his home and see Emma's room at the ranch. It was full of things like trophies that Emma had won as a teenager. And a saddle still graced the corner of the room. He'd meant to ask Emma about it but hadn't gotten around to it as yet.

"That's my mom." Darin looked at the woman and felt like someone had punched him in the head. "Isn't she really pretty? I think she's upset though. Miss Susie showed her that you're not real."

"Not real?" Bonnie nodded and pulled him along to meet her mom. He stopped her before they got very far. "Honey, what do you mean, not real?"

"That you're a great big cat." Darin looked around at the rest of his family, then back at the woman. She *was* upset. And more than that, she looked ready to bolt. His cat stirred along his skin, reminding him that he really was a great big cat and that he needed to comfort Mrs. Crosby. "Mom, this is Darin. He's the owner of this this place. And he and Mr. Truman made me lunch today."

"And what is Mr. Truman? A cat too? Or is he a...I don't know. A vampire perhaps?" Christ, she was beautiful, and being pissed off like she was made her all the more gorgeous. For some reason, Darin thought it was funny.

"No. He's an elite shifter. Which means he can shift into anything. The only vampire I have working here is the night watchman. He's not able to come in this early. I think he needed to drain a few dozen people before he came to work." He saw her sway a little just as his aunt popped him in the back of the head. He felt horrible for what he'd said and that he'd made her more upset. "I'm sorry. I should have been nicer about that. I'm guessing that you don't think you've had a lot of contact with our kind before."

"No, I have not." When she reached for Bonnie, who dodged her mother's hand, Darin wanted to tell her again how sorry he was. "Bonnie, come here. I think we should leave."

"Because you have your panties in a twist? Or is it because you're seeing something that you don't understand?" He knew that his brother was getting angry with him for talking out of turn, but for some reason he wanted to see her pissed, not upset. He leaned closer to her to see what other shifters she'd been around in the last hour and nearly fell forward. Her scent. It was.... It was all he could do not to pull her body to his.

"Darin?" He looked at his brother and realized that his cat was purring along his skin. Jace told him twice to control him, and it was all Darin could to not to shift and take the woman. "Darin? Damn it. What's wrong with you?"

"She smells like sex." The slap across his face had him grabbing the woman and pulling her to his body. She was furious, and his cat wanted to mark her. Burying his nose at her throat, Darin was aware on some level that he was scaring her and that his family was right there. When he moved back, but didn't let go, he looked at Mason. "She's my mate. I can smell it on her."

"Well, shit." He looked at Aunt Georgie when she cursed and cocked his brow at her. "You boys are going to be the death of me. You know that, don't you? Mercedes, honey, I'm sorry about this, but my nephew here is your mate. I know that you have no idea what that means, but if we can go in the dining room now, I'm sure that I can make you understand."

"I don't think so. I want to know why he thinks I smell like sex. And what the hell does that even smell like?" Darin felt his cat rub along his skin, and he knew that she could feel him too. "What was that? Are you going to turn into something?"

"My cat. He wants to touch you." When she struggled to be let go, he did, but not without some pain from his cat. "I need to touch you or he's going to come out. And if he does, then you're going to run and he's going to think it's a game. I believe my aunt is right. We should go and have some dinner and we'll talk when this is finished."

"No. No. I don't want to talk to you. I want to know what is going on." Darin tried to hold his cat, but she was upset and he wanted her to be calm. Touching his hand to her arm, Darin felt his cat calm little by little. "You have to back off. You're scaring me."

"He's not going to hurt you, but you have to let me touch you. I'm sorry. I know this is a lot, but I promise you this is the best way." He could see that she was freaked out. Well, he was as well. "I'm a cougar. And we're not going to hurt you. Ever. You have to believe me when I say that to you."

"I want to go home. Please. I want to go back home." Darin didn't bother telling her that wherever she went from now on, he was going too. As he guided her to the dining room, the rest of his family followed. No one said a word as they moved to be seated. "I can't be here. I just want to go home."

"I promise you, Mercedes, I'll tell you whatever you want to know about us. Just don't run or leave us. If you do, then he's going to come after you. Not to hurt you, but he's bigger and sometimes very clumsy." Mason laughed across from him. "You're not helping."

"I'm not, I'm sure, but you should tell her what happens if she runs. I don't want that any more than you do." She asked him what happened. "You call his cat. I mean, he will shift and while he won't hurt you, it will hurt him a great deal."

It wouldn't, but before he could correct his brother, Jace touched his mind. *She won't run if she thinks you'll be hurt. At least I hope not. Just let her think that for the time being and we'll deal with this as it comes. Right now we're here to have dinner. And to invite her and her little girl...well, I guess into the family.*

Christ, I don't need this right now. Jace asked him what he meant. *I have too much shit on my plate as it is. This place and the men coming in tomorrow. I'm supposed to go out and show her the...mother fuck. I have a daughter.*

No, she has a daughter. And until she's willing to share her with you, then you are nothing to her. Darin started to argue. *If you don't believe me. then by all means, tell her that her daughter is yours. I'm telling you right now that I will help her when she runs. Because, big brother, she will do that to protect the only person in the world she loves.*

"What does this mate thing involve? And if you tell me that it means that I'm subservient to you, then you can shove that shit right up your ass. I'm not doing that again." Darin glanced at his brother and then looked at her when she continued. "And my little girl, what happens to her now that you think that you have some sort of claim over me?"

"My name is Darin. Darin Douglas." He put out his hand, and she only stared at it. "I have no idea of your name. Other than Crosby. And if you don't mind, I'd really like to start over." She eyed him and his hand, and he was sure she wasn't going to take it. "I'm sorry for before. I'm not...well, to be honest, I'm not sure that's not normal when one of us finds our mate. You're my first and only one."

"I've heard that before, that I belonged to someone. And when he came home in a shitty mood, he hit me. Actually, he could be in any sort of mood. When the need to slap or punch came over him, he'd do it. Then he threatened to kill me or my little girl if I so much as tried to leave him." Darin looked at Bonnie, who was talking to his aunt. "You hurt her, or even look like you're going to, then I will kill you. Not a threat, Mr. Douglas, but you can count on it." He looked at her.

She was ferocious, angry, and hurt. Confused as well, but then so was he. And she was protective. Not of herself but of her daughter. And Jace had been right. She would never be his, not ever, if he didn't do right by them both.

"No one will ever hurt you again. Either of you. For as long as I live, I will do everything within my power to not only protect the two of you, but to love you with all that I am. Provide for you both. My family, too, will be there for you when no one else will. We will stand beside you, no matter if we agree with you or not, but we're your family and will do all that we can to make sure that you are never alone again." She looked around the room when he did, at all of them staring at her. Then she looked back at him. "This is a promise that I make to you on my life."

"No one is that nice." He smiled at her. "This is...it's too much. I don't know what to believe."

"I can understand that. And thank you." She asked him for what. "For not telling me to screw off. For not saying that you simply didn't believe me. Mostly for letting my cat calm enough that I can eat."

He kissed her hand and put it in his lap. Darin wanted her to leave it there, to hold onto his thigh, to give him some comfort too. And when she didn't pull away, he reached into his jacket pocket and pulled out his notepad and pen. He noticed that Jessie did the same. It was time for work.

~~~

The dinner was wonderful. After a little while, Mercedes started to relax enough to talk to everyone. They were loud and mean to each other, but mostly she could see that they truly did love one another. When the dinner plates were taken away, she watched both Jessie and Darin write something down and she asked him about it.

"This was a trial run for the kitchen. To make notes on what we need to do when guests arrive. Truman, the chef, asked that we make notes on things we saw that might need improvement, as well as anything that we liked. So far my column on liking things is longer than the improvements side." He handed her his list. "Tell me what you would put on it."

"Me? I have no idea." Mason, as the other side of the table laughed, asked her if she ate out. "Of course. Nothing this fancy, but yes, Bonnie and I go out sometimes."

"Then tell us what you would suggest. I have one. More of a question really. What happens if all the guests want to have dinner at the same time? I mean, this is really nice and large enough for us to talk, but there are nine suites, right?" Jessie laughed and told them there were only six now. "Six? I thought there were nine floors." Jessie said he wanted to answer that one.

"There are. But we decided that at some point we were going to run into a kind of situation that you just mentioned. So Darin thought we should have separate dining areas. The third floor is set up like this one, with a temporary bar as well as a dumbwaiter to take the food up and down. He also had a heat room put in, a place to put the food while it's being readied to serve." Jessie looked at Darin. "Tell them about the sixth floor."

"It's really not that big a deal. But we made it into a sort of working dining area. There are projector screens on three of the walls that hide away. Also, while the dining won't be as extensive as the other two places, there is a bar that is much larger that also can be used as a buffet if necessary." Mercedes noticed that he never once said I did this or that, but said we. When he turned to her, she smiled at him. "Really, I'd like to know what you would do differently."

Mercedes looked at the table and decided to go with it. "The flowers are too much. In order to see around them, you have to dodge them. Perhaps if you were to make a flat display or none at all, you could put the tall vases around the room with lighting." When he wrote it down, she felt silly.

"This is good. Yes, you're right. I have been trying to see Aunt Georgie at the other end but wasn't seeing that it was the flowers. And I do like the more lighting idea too." Jessie was writing things down. "What else?"

"The salad dressing is okay, but the lettuce is weird. What happened to the green stuff we had today?" Mercedes started to tell Bonnie that was rude when Georgie agreed with her. "Can you have different kinds? When Mom and I went out for my birthday one time, they brought us three different kinds in little bowls."

As ideas and comments were tossed around the table, the chef came out to hear them too. The dessert cart was also brought out, and she could see that someone had gone to a great deal of effort to make a large yet beautiful variety of things to choose from. Mercedes had the lemon tart and a blueberry buckle when she was told this, too, was a taste effort.

"I like the tart, but the buckle is my favorite." Truman told her that the pack alpha-bitch had made them. "Excuse me?"

"That's what they're called. Her name is Julia Sexton. Her husband is Paddy. I heard you saw him today." She remembered the big wolf and nodded at Darin when he spoke softly to her. "Mason is the oldest of us boys, so he's our leader. And we're called a leap. Or sometimes an ambush. And since Mason is our leader, that makes Emma his bitch. It's not meant to be mean. It's just what we're called."

"I don't care for it." Darin nodded and smiled at her. "What are you called? I mean as a brother, what is your title?"

He leaned into her throat, and she felt her body heat up, her pussy swell with need, and the dampness made her squirm on her seat. And when he nipped at her earlobe, it was all she could do not to moan. Darin took her hand in his, and when he curled his fingers into hers, all Mercedes could think about was being naked with this man, feeling him touch her body. Making love to him in a soft and loving way. And when he pulled away, she gripped his hand tightly in hers and looked at him.

"I've never...what was that?" Her voice was low, full of some emotion that she had no name for.

"Just me. Tasting you." It was on the tip of her tongue to beg him to taste her again. Everywhere. But someone down the table said his name, and he turned to them. Mercedes was glad for the break.

"It gets better." Mercedes looked at Holly when she spoke. "The sex is fantastic. And all consuming. But they really do love you with all that they are. And family isn't just a word to them, but an actual way of life when it comes to being together. Any of them would die for the other without a moment's hesitation."

"He's a cat. A shifter." Holly nodded. "So are you, they told me. And you're going to have a baby by one of them. Aren't you afraid of what it will be?"

"No. It's not like that, and that's a good question. Up until they're older, they're just a baby like all of them are. They'll heal a lot faster. Never get ill, and they're stronger too." Holly rubbed her belly, and Mercedes wanted to do the same. "Children born to this family will never feel as if they don't belong. And ones brought in, like your daughter, will never feel as if she's not an equal part of this crew either. Darin will love you like no man ever has, protect you and Bonnie as he said he would, and you will never have a family quite like this one."

"I don't want to be a part of this or any family. I've had my fill of relationships." Holly only nodded. "You think you can convince me. Or he does. But I'm not going to fall for anything anymore. I don't have just me to take care of, but my daughter as well. And now my dad. I won't be hurt again by a man."

"And you won't." Mercedes said nothing but watched them around the table. Truman was teased about things, and like the rest of the family, he took it and gave back as well. When they were asked to rate their dinner on a scale of one to ten, she was almost afraid what they'd tell him. Mason started it out.

"I have to give you an eight. I loved the steak, but I think that the baked potato could have been a little more. Maybe, I don't know, with chives or bacon or something. It was somewhat boring." Truman nodded, making his own notes. "There wasn't any bread either."

"Oh shit." When he ran to the kitchen and returned with an armload of baskets filled with breadsticks, everyone laughed and took some of it. "I had it out on the table earlier, but took it off so that I could serve it with the warmed butter. Completely forgot it."

"These are delicious. So now I'll give you a nine. But I stand on my decision about the potato." Mason snagged two more pieces of bread when Holly spoke.

"I liked that there were pitchers of water on the table. And lemon slices hanging on the side of it should you want them. The steak was wonderful and, like Mason, I think the potato was sort of a little boring. Not boring, but sort of normal. Also, I absolutely loved the salad, but again, I think you could have given more choices, as Bonnie said." Holly looked at Mercedes. "Other than the flowers, what did you love or hate about the dinner?"

"I personally love baked potatoes. And would have enjoyed bacon on it, and sour cream. Chives? Not really. But some real green onions would have been great." Truman explained the lack of onions. "Oh. I never thought of that. Onion breath in a conference room. Good thinking then. The dessert trolley was a wonderful touch, with so many varieties that it was difficult to choose from. If I were you, I'd put two on a plate or when someone picks, encourage them to have a second one. That would win me over."

The rest of them had ideas and small things that they said might have needed to be improved upon. All of them were kind about it, always had positive along with the negative. Georgie suggested lowering the volume of the background music. It had been a little loud. Logan said that the wait staff needed to be friendlier and not quite so stiff. Even Bonnie suggested that they have maybe a veggie tray on the table for those of them that couldn't wait for more food.

"For you, my dear, I will do that. I don't care for the green and leafy myself, but I am sure that as a human, you would." She smiled at him, and Mercedes realized it had been a very long time since her little girl looked that happy. "And I will dig out the dressing servers. Do you have a suggestion on those as well? I am open for anything."

"Not that stinky stuff that Mom likes. Bleu cheese is nasty. But I was thinking French. I love that. And maybe something...I don't know. I just like French." Truman wrote down what she said, and Mercedes smiled at them. "Mom and I went to this really fancy place for her birthday one time. They had hot croutons. They were really good. I could have just eaten them. But they had this white cheese on them that the waitress cut up on it, grated I mean. That was really good too."

"Fresh croutons." Everyone agreed that might be a nice treat. "And I was thinking on the potato situation. I had this recipe for twice baked ones. They have bacon and cheese already in them. Would that be better, you think?"

By the time they were ready to go, Truman had found several things that he wanted to try in the future. It was agreed upon that they'd be his testers for future dinners and anytime he wanted to send something to them. Mercedes decided that if she stayed here too long, she'd need to go on a major diet. This job might prove to be very fattening.

CHAPTER 5

Darin wanted to take her home with him, but he also knew that would be a huge mistake. First of all, there was Bonnie to think of, and secondly, she didn't believe in him. Not the cat part, but as a man in general. He was going to have to tread slowly or have her run. When he walked her to Mason's car, he stood by while her daughter was put in the back seat, then asked to speak to Mercedes for a moment.

"I was wondering if you'd allow me to kiss you." She shook her head. "All right. Then how about if you kiss me? I'll keep my hands to myself, I promise."

"Funny. But I don't want to get into something that will hurt me or Bonnie." He nodded understanding, of course, but wanted more. "You and your family are really nice, Darin, but I'm not alone in this."

"No, you're not. And while I understand, I can still hope, can't I?" He wanted to touch her, bring her into his arms and tell her that everything was going to be perfect. But he knew better. Somewhere out there was her ex, and he was going to be a problem for them. "I'll see you tomorrow then. I have to be here early, but I was going to go by the ranches on my way in."

"I have to go into town too, later in the afternoon tomorrow. I want to look into the school that Mason suggested. He said it was safe." Darin told her it was. "Why does he feel that it's safer than the one that she was at before? I mean, it was a private school and I trusted the staff there."

"This school is run by the pack for the pack." Mercedes backed up and he felt her fear. "No, don't do that. You were doing so well before. But the pack, a pack of wolves, knows who she is and who you are. You know of Julia, and Bonnie seemed to enjoy talking to both her and her sister Candace. She's a teacher there as well. They'll protect her as you would, lay down their life for her and the other children, because they know that children are all we have for our future."

"Easy words to say, but I don't want her taken." Darin assured her that no one would dare go there with any intent to harm anyone or they'd pay for it with their lives. "And why is that? What makes you think that they'd kill for a stranger?"

He wanted to tell her that it was patrolled by the best men there were. But he knew also that she'd not believe him. So Darin put his fingers in his mouth and whistled. No one moved as the pack that kept them safe at all times came out of the darkness. When she curled her body around his, Darin held her as he spoke.

"This is what would greet them should they try to take even a backpack that didn't belong to them. Paddy and his pack are around all the time. As some of our leap is around when they are out and about as humans. No one will see them unless they want them to." Paddy came up to her and sat down. "He wants to taste your skin. Not hurt you, but should you ever need him to find you, he can."

"He did that to Bonnie. Today when they were in the yard. He licked her hand." Darin wasn't there, but he said that had been it. "I don't understand any of this. I'm overwhelmed and feel like at any moment something terrible is going to happen."

Darin took her hand in his and put it out for Paddy. When he licked it, the big wolf took off and he turned Mercedes so that she faced him. His body was close enough to her now that he could feel her heat, smell her arousal, and touch her should he like, but he only stared at her.

"Touch me." She shook her head but didn't move away from him. "Feel my pulse and know that it beats for you. I want to taste your flesh. Feel your pulse as it beats under my tongue. Bite you hard enough to draw your flavor into my mouth, drink from you in a way that has you screaming out my name in pleasure. I want all of that and more. But I won't. Not until you're ready. Not until you tell me you want me."

"I'm afraid." He said that he was as well. "But you're this big bad cat. You can take on a man and be done with him. I'm only me and Bonnie, and I'm terrified that you'll hurt me."

Stepping back from her was the hardest thing he'd ever done. And when she stood there, he took another step back. His cat was pissed, running along his skin painfully. Shaking his body, he smiled at her.

"I live on the McBride ranch. I'm not sure if I'm going to change the name or not, but that's where I am should you ever need me. And I don't mean just sexually either." Her face heated up, and he could see it glowing in the moonlight. "I'm not ever going to lie to you, but I have to go now. I need a good hard run with my cat."

"I've never seen your cat." He only nodded. "I might not ever be to the point where I want to have sex with you. I'm not even sure I like you overly much."

Pulling her into his arms, he kissed her, giving her all the pent-up sexual frustration that he could. When he let her go, he was pleased to see her stagger back. He was unsteady himself. Without a word, he turned on his heel and walked away. Darin thought perhaps it was the most difficult thing he'd ever done or ever would do again.

Stripping down to his pants, he kicked his shoes under his truck and let his cat take him. His pants would be ruined, but at the moment he didn't give a shit. The woods were calling to him almost as hard as his body needed Mercedes.

He ran for about an hour. He knew that both Logan and Gerard had tried to contact him, but he wasn't in a good place right now, and he had to do this or hurt someone. One of his brothers might have fought him for a couple of rounds, but he needed more. Sitting on the edge of the pond, he heard someone coming up behind him and was surprised to find Landon walking in the dark woods.

"If you don't mind, I'd enjoy sitting with you for a spell." Darin laid his head down on his paws, and Landon sat down beside him and curled his arm around his waist. The two of them had exchanged a little blood so they could talk when they needed to. "You know, I sometimes wish I had been a big cat like you boys. Not often, mind, but a few times. I might have killed my son though, and that kinda makes me glad that I'm not."

You wouldn't have been able to live with yourself had you done that. You're a good man, Landon. Landon said he wouldn't have been able to stand it at that. *What are you doing out here? I thought old men like you went to bed with the sun.*

"Don't be an ass." They both laughed. "I came out here to see if you were all right. Mason said that girl is your mate. I thought the two of you would be breaking in that new house of yours."

She doesn't trust me. Landon nodded but didn't say anything for a moment. *I'm not sure what to do to have her trust me. I'm a good person. I'd never hurt her or Bonnie.*

"That other man, her ex, he done a number on her. I heard something about it. Had me a private eye, are they still called that? Anyway, I had me one of them private dicks go out and find me out a few things. Want me to share with you?" He wasn't sure and said so. "This'll help you, I think. And I want to help you, Darin. Of all the boys, you Douglas boys, I find you to be the closest to me. Like the son I wished I had."

They sat there, the two of them, in silence. Darin wasn't sure what was going on in Landon's mind, but he knew that it had to do with his son. Dirk had tried to kill his own father before he'd died. It had been a horrific time, dealing with the son of the man he'd come to love. Remembering something that he'd thought of last week, he told his dear friend.

Mason and I were a few years older than Emma and Dirk. But we knew him. Not a lot about your daughter. She sort of stayed to herself. I thought then she was being a snob, but I think she was just different than the rest of us. Better. Landon just leaned on him more in answer. *One afternoon I was walking toward the ranch when I saw Dirk on the side of the road. He wasn't hurt or anything, just sitting there. Like he was waiting on someone. Then this little girl comes around the street corner where he was.*

"Please don't tell me he hurt her. I'm not sure I can handle that today, Darin." He assured him that he hadn't. "All right then. You tell me your story. Then I'll tell you mine."

The little girl was pushing her bike. The chain had come off or something. I don't remember that part. But Dirk stood up and helped her with it. He didn't hurt her or tease her for having a broken down bike, but helped her out and then held onto her bag while she rode it up and down the street. I think he was making sure that it was going to work for her. Landon sniffled, and Darin continued. *When they were both satisfied that it was all right, he helped her put her bag on the handle bars and she drove off. Dirk moved in the opposite direction, looking back once in a while until she was out of sight.*

There was more to the story, but Darin wasn't going to tell him that. How several days later, on the same street corner, Dirk had tripped her up. Not just knocked her off the bike, but had bloodied her arm and nose too. And when she cried about what he'd done, he'd kicked her twice and told her to fuck off. That part of the story more suited the type of person Dirk the Dick had been, but Landon wasn't going to hear that from him.

"Thank you, son. You have no idea what that does for me. Knowing that somewhere in his heart he was a good boy. And that I'd not failed him completely." Darin told him he hadn't failed him at all. "Nash Crosby is a mean son of a bitch. I mean, you might have guessed that, but you've no idea how bad he is. And he wants that little family of yours to heel to him. He's coming here. He knows she's here."

Mason has someone tagging him. I guess he's been asking around where she lived to find out as much as he can. Landon said it was more than that. *What do you mean?*

"He's killed two people. The man that lived across from her, the one he had spying on her, is dead. Hanged in his own bathroom by his own guts. And a woman that worked in her office. Milly someone. I don't think she was able to keep whatever information she might have had from him. He did a number on her and her poor body." Landon shivered as he continued. "He also knows about her daddy, and that she'd lied to him about his whereabouts. Smart girl, your mate. She kept him in the dark for a long time. But now he's powerfully pissed off."

We'll protect her. You know that, don't you? Landon said that he did know that. Better than most. *What else? I'm sure there's more.*

"Yes." Landon stretched out his legs and was quiet for a moment before he told him the rest. "He's got him a crew. Men that are as mean as Dirk was, but more controlled about it. My buddy said that these men that are coming with him, they're not like regular criminals but hardened ones. Man by the name of Bends keeps them in line and is the right hand to that feller, Crosby. Don't rightly know his first name, but it's in my notes at home. These men are the kind that'll tear your eyes out of your head should you look at them wrong. Or even if they think you looked at them wrong."

He leaned over then and pulled a thick envelope out of his back pocket. He laid it in front of him, and Darin was afraid to ask him what was in it. As they sat there, quiet again, Darin thought of the kind of person Dirk had been and wondered how these men could be any worse. Landon rubbed him behind the ears as he continued.

"He has no use for Bonnie. A boy might have been different for him, but with her being a girl child, he'll kill her right off if he can't find any use for her. Or he'll use her a little to get to the mom, but she don't have to be alive for Mercedes to think that he has her." Darin said nothing, his body stiff with fear for the two of them. "He's hurt her before, the little one. Broke her leg trying to get her to get out of the car when he'd found her ride to and from school when she was younger. Just snapped it like it wasn't nothing more than a bothersome thing to get what he wanted. Had the police not been called...well, I don't even want to think about what he might have done to her. Or her momma to get her back to him. He's a might on the possessive side, but I think it's a tad more than that. Not that he loves her, but simply because he feels she belongs to him."

I have to talk to her. Tell her what we've found out. Make her understand that we're going to be here for the two of them. Landon said that was his best bet. *And I have to try and make her understand that she's only as safe as she can be if she lets us help her.*

"I'm not saying that it's gonna be an easy job for you. Nope, I don't think it's gonna be, but I will tell you that you'd better move fast. He's coming here and he's not going to stop until someone stops him. Permanently." Darin agreed with him. "You get your stuff together, son, and I'll be here should you need me. You know that. But these old bones are hurting a little, and I need to go to my own warm bed and wife."

After Landon left him, Darin sat there for an hour or so more. The sun was just coming up when he made his way into his house. There wasn't much point in him going to bed, but he did shower and get ready for his day. The envelope was on the bottom of his bed when he realized that he hadn't looked at its contents. Opening it up, he realized something else. He was going to need help. And a great deal of it.

But first he had to speak to Mercedes. Darin was sure that it was going to be harder to talk to her than it was getting ready for his first customer today. Christ, he thought, he was going to be so fucked.

~~~

Mercedes watched the ponies. They were the most gorgeous creatures she'd ever seen. They were wild and tame at the same time, and she wanted more than anything to walk up to one and touch it. Susie had told her that first she needed to be accepted by the big guy, Bride, as he went by. But Christ, he was fucking huge.

"Just put out your hand so that he can smell you." Mercedes nodded and put out her hand slowly to the black mustang. "He's not going to hurt you. I mean, he might have if you'd just have come into his home where his ladies are, but he won't while I'm here."

"This is like the wolf last night, right? Get my scent and he can find me anywhere?" Susie laughed and the big horse perked up his ears. "I can't believe I'm doing this. This is not what I thought I'd be doing."

"Bride will either accept you or not, but you can't go near his harras without his approval. He might let you help them, but he won't allow you to come and go without one of us being around." Mercedes waited for him to touch his nose to her hand. When he did, his lips nibbling on her like he really was tasting her, she put out the apple that she had when Susie told her to. Then he did the most extraordinary thing…he put his head to hers. "Congratulations. You are now a member of his harras, Mercedes."

She felt…well, accepted. And as the tears filled her eyes, she ran her fingers down his flanks to his back and up to his neck. The horse was an amazing animal. He seemed to be in excellent shape too. As she was looking him over, a truck pulled in the drive and she didn't bother looking up. Her entire being was focused on the animal in front of her.

"You touch me that way and I'll die a happy man." She glanced over at Darin but didn't speak to him. To be honest, she was trying to make her mouth work and wasn't able to do it.

She decided that it was the hat. All of them wore them, some black, others tan. Some that looked like they'd been dragged behind a horse and others still that had a fresh look to them. The black one that sat on his head made her think of ropes and whips. Of him making love to her in nothing but the stupid hat. And when he tipped it back, as he did now, she wanted to drop to her knees and beg him to take her.

"I can smell you, Mercedes. Do you have any idea how much I love that you're aroused right now? That I want to do to you whatever things are going on in your head." He cleared his throat and took in a deep breath before letting it out again. "I'd like to talk to you when you're done. It's really important."

"So is this." The big horse moved away from her when she patted him on the backside. "And so you know, I'm not ever touching you that way."

"If you say so." His grin was just too charming, and she was pretty sure that he knew it. "I've been looking into a few things. Mostly about your ex. I wanted to come by and let you know what we've been able to find out."

"Is he here?" He told her not yet but he was coming. "I see. And when he gets here, do you have any idea what he'll do to your family when he finds out just where I am?"

"We're ready for him. And so you know, he does know just where you are." She felt her knees shake and was glad that the fence was close enough that she could grab it. "Are you ready for this, or do you want me to give it to you in bits and pieces?"

"I don't know. Is it really bad?" He nodded, and she knew deep in her heart that he was telling her the truth. "Who did he kill?"

"I'm sorry, honey, but he killed the man across from you at your apartment. Your neighbor, Mr. Jacks. The police are still looking into it, but he was...his murder could not have been easy on him. They don't know what he might have known, but he was hanged by his own intestine. Milly is gone as well, the woman from the office where you worked. They're not releasing her name until they find her family to notify them." She nodded and gripped tighter on the post in front of her. "Mercedes, I'm going to take you into the house and set you down. I'm going to put my arms around you, all right?"

"I'm terrified." He said he knew that, that he could actually feel it. "He's not going to stop, is he? He's going to come here and kill everyone, and even then it won't be enough. He's a horrible...I was going to say horrible human being, but he's not even that. He's a monster."

"He won't hurt you. I've made sure that there are extra patrols around the school, too, where Bonnie is going to go. Emma and Mason are watching her, as well as the pack. No one will get to her." She nodded and felt his arms as they moved around her. "Come on, love. Let me take you inside where you can sit down."

She moved with him. It felt both comforting and safe to be in his arms. As she was seated on the couch he started to stand up, and she grabbed his hands and held them in hers. For reasons that she couldn't fathom right now, she needed his touch.

"Just don't leave me right now. I need to tell you about him. What he did to me. He held a gun to my head when he made me marry him. First he shot the man standing there that was in the room with us. He wanted me to know that the gun was loaded and what it would do once he had to fire it into me. I had blood on my face when he shot the man. Nash told me that he'd kill my father too if I ran. Kill my poor father who knew nothing about him." Mercedes was handed something cold and told to drink it. As she sipped the sweet tea, she cried harder. "I couldn't even take my daughter out for her birthday for fear that he'd find us. He would have too. Just walk up to anyone with us and blow their heads off to make me mind him. I can't do that anymore, Darin. I just can't do this."

"I have you now. You're going to be safe." She shook her head. "You will. I will die for you."

"You don't know what sort of monster he is. You have no idea what he's capable of." He said nothing, and she looked at him. Really looked. "You're so handsome. I bet you have women falling all over you all the time, don't you? Why me? Why do you think I'm your mate? I'm nothing but trouble and heartache."

He kissed her mouth, gently and softly. And when he moved his mouth along her chin to her throat, she leaned back when he gave her just a little push. Her body was warmed by his. He held her in a way that made her feel loved, safe, and beautiful. When he lifted his head from hers, she stared at him, touched her fingers to his mouth as he had her lips.

"You have to tell me what you want." She told him that she wanted him. "No, that's not what I mean and you know it. Do you want me in your life? Because if we make love right now, it's going to be forever. I'm going to be your mate for all time. Do you understand that? Forever, Mercedes. I'll never leave you. Never hurt you or Bonnie. I belong to you."

"You mean I belong to you." He shook his head. "I don't understand. You say I'm your mate, but you don't want me."

"Oh, I want you. Never doubt that. I would like nothing more than to take you right here right now. Taste parts of you and make you moan. Nibble on your nipples until you beg me to bite you. I want to bury my cock deep inside of you, make love to you hard and fast one moment, then slowly and reverently the next. I want you as no man has ever wanted you." Mercedes told him to take her then. "I can't take you, Mercedes. You have to want me to. I want you to say that you understand that this, this thing between us, is forever. I don't want you to ever feel that I pressured you into this. I would hate myself if you ever felt like I did anything to you that you didn't want or need as badly as I do. And I do want you."

"I want to feel loved." He said that he did love her. "You can't love me, Darin. We don't even know each other."

"But I do. And if you really think on it, you believe me too. And I know a great deal about you. I know that you're an amazing mother and mom. You put your little girl ahead of anyone, including yourself. You're smart and funny. You've been hurt more than you should have ever been." He kissed her then, a quick touching of their mouths. Then he sat back on his knees again. "Christ, what I wouldn't do to have you naked and spread out like this before me. Or bent over the back of the couch while I take you that way. Eat you until I have my fill, which may take days to get enough of you."

"I need you." He touched his fingers to her pussy, and she moaned. "Please, I need to feel you inside of me."

"Not today. I have to go to work, and there are any number of people outside waiting on you to come to work again." She rode his fingers as he thumbed her clit. "Ride me until you come. Then I'm going to taste your blood."

His mouth was over her breasts, and she lifted her blouse up for him to taste her. When she felt his breath on her breast, it was all she could do to not beg him to make her come. She rode his hand while he gave her such pleasure. And when he bit down hard on her breast, she rose up off the couch with a scream as she came.

"Christ, baby. Again, come again for me." There was no slow buildup this time, her body detonated quickly and loudly. When he took her mouth, Mercedes reached for his cock as he continued to fuck her through her clothing, and she slid her hand into his pants to feel him.

He was thick and hot. The tip of him was wet, and she wanted to taste him. Having him rock into her palm wasn't enough. Her need for this man was out of control, and she had a feeling that his was just as bad.

"Take me. Fill me." He was shaking his head. "Take me now, Darin, or so help me I will hurt you."

He pulled his pants to his knees and made short work of hers. When she was naked from the waist down, her blouse up over her breasts, as was her bra, he leaned over her and took her still bare breast into his mouth. His cock was at her entrance. She could feel each time he slid his crown into her, like he was giving her small heart attacks with each stroke.

"When I take you, we're one." She nodded, anything to have him fill her like she needed. "Forever, Mercedes. I belong to no one but you."

"Please, just take me." He brought her hips to the edge of the couch and slammed forward to fill her like no one had before. And when he pulled her up off the cushion, Mercedes wrapped her legs around his waist and held on. His cock didn't just fill her, but felt like a part of her.

His hands and mouth were everywhere. It felt as if he burned her, seared her skin each time his fingers only brushed over her. His mouth felt hotter. His teeth grazed her flesh like he was memorizing each part of her for taste and texture. When he cupped her ass, bringing her as close to him as she could get, Mercedes threw back her head, letting him touch the pulse at her throat that even she could feel pounding.

Laying her on the floor, he never took his eyes from hers. She felt as if she could see every part of him, inside and out. All the way to his soul and beyond. And when he made love to her, making love to all of her and not just her body, she knew in that moment that she had fallen in love with him, and it frightened her more than anything had before.

"Stay with me, love. Look at me." Her eyes had closed, and she opened them now to see him again. "I love you. I need to taste you. Give me your throat and I'll give you mine."

"Don't hurt me." He assured her she'd enjoy it. "I know, but later. I don't want you to hurt me, please, Darin? I can't stand it if you hurt me."

"Never." His mouth moved to her pounding pulse at her throat again, his teeth making her body warmer, wetter for him. It was all she could do to hold on to her pending climax. She had no idea why, but she knew that when he bit her and her him, it was going to be the best climax she'd ever had, or ever would have. As soon as he started to pound her, his cock pistoling in her, she dug her nails into his back and bit down on his shoulder when he told her now. His own teeth tore into her savagely.

Nothing could have prepared her for the feelings that hit her. Not just hers but his as well. He filled her, her mind and her body. His thoughts were hers, and she was sure that he could see hers as well. As he took her over the edge again, it was almost too much, and not enough at the same time. They were one, and would be for the rest of her days. She knew this now.

CHAPTER 6

Leaving her had been hard, but he'd been called three times in the last ten minutes and he had to go or stay all day. As he made his way into his office at the Douglas House, he was stopped by Jessie. He had no idea what he might have been going to say, but he paused when he was close enough to no doubt smell Mercedes on him.

"I guess I understand now." Darin only nodded. "I'm really sorry, but the Rose party will be here in less than an hour and there's a problem."

"What sort of problem? And please tell me that we can fix it." When Jessie didn't answer him, Darin knew it was bad. "Tell me."

"Truman's been beaten. He's in the hospital now and they're not sure that he's going to make it. And before you ask, yes, he's getting the best of care, and I've had two men put on him in the event that someone returns to finish him off." Darin asked him if they knew who it was. "I don't, but I think the police know. He managed to kill one of them before they got away. And I think they left enough information behind that you might be able to send some trackers out for them. And so you know, when I couldn't get in touch with you, I had to call Mason."

"Good. I'm glad and I'm sorry, but I needed her." Jessie said he understood. "What did Mason say?"

"He's sent a man to the hospital as well. This one, he said, can find anyone, and I believed him." Jessie sat down in the chair across from him. "As for the Rose party, that's all ready. I don't know what we'll do about food for them, but I guess we'll cross that when we need to. For the most part, everything for the late snacks is done. But dinner will be a problem."

"Call the pack and tell Paddy what's going on, and ask him if Julia and a couple more women can come in and help us out until we can get things figured out. Thank goodness we only have one in the place for now." Jessie said that there were calls coming in to make reservations, but he'd been putting them off until they had a set date. "Good, that way we can put off until we have things settled here. Truman has a son. I think he lives with him. Can you go and see if either of them need anything and make sure they have it?"

"All right. Anything else?" Darin said off the top of his head no but to call the pack. "I'll call now. And when I find out, I'll let you know.

Darin knew that Mason would call him when he found anything out, but called him on his cell to let him know that he and Mercedes had mated and bonded. As leap leader, he had to know these things. His brother congratulated him and told him then what he knew.

"The man that was killed is from Vegas. Just a short hop from where Mercedes lived. I'm not one-hundred percent sure, but I'm betting that this is the work of her ex." Darin said he didn't doubt it. "I just heard from the hospital, and they're saying that Truman is going to make it, but he's going to be down for a while. He's too weak to shift, but once he is stronger they think he'll be fine."

"Great. I'm so glad to hear that. Jessie said they weren't giving him good odds before." He thought of Mercedes and Bonnie. "I'm going to ask her to move in with me. I think she'll be safer there for the simple reason that the house is set so far back from everything else that we'll have plenty of warning before they get to us. Not to mention I'd feel better if she was not with Emma in her condition. Not that I don't think she can care for herself, I just don't trust this guy not to hurt her to get to Mercedes."

"You might be right. And I talked to Landon too. He said he showed you some things at the house that will keep you safe as well." Landon had shown him a great many things at the house that he'd bet he'd not even shared with his wife. "But I'd ask her, not demand."

"I got that." Mason said that he knew he had but wanted to be sure. "There is a shelter in place, one of those lockdown rooms in our bedroom, as well as in the one that Bonnie will be in. I'm not sure about where Dirk lived because Landon can't go in there, but I'm betting there is one there too. Also a tunnel under the house that has this huge fucking room in it. It'll open out in a field about two miles from the house. There is enough food for a pretty long standoff should it come to that. Landon was a man who protected his family. But about Mercedes...I'm in love with her. I don't think she believes me, but I am. Christ, I never thought that it could feel so consuming and not enough at the same time to love someone."

"Wait until she has a baby. I cannot tell you how many times a day I go and search for Emma so I can see her belly roll. And to hear her say that she loves me." Darin leaned back in his chair, just realizing that he'd had no sleep at all last night. "Darin, she's going to be safe with us. Everyone at all three ranches, they're watching out for her and Bonnie. Who I must say I have fallen in love with too."

"I have to be here for today. The Rose group is coming in at two, and I still need to figure out about a cook." Jessie came to the door and gave him the thumbs up with a note that said she's coming. "Well, okay, the cook part is taken care of. Thank goodness for pack."

"Julia?" Darin said it was. "You'll have to think of something to give Paddy for this. I know that you'll pay his wife and whoever works for you, but he'll need homage. It's only right."

Yawning, he told him that he'd do it. "Mason, do you think it ever becomes normal? I mean, our lives. Does anything ever just become every day? Right now I could use some normal."

"I have no idea what normal means. A year ago we were struggling to not lose the farm and not end up in jail. Now not only do I have enough money to buy and sell this town ten times over, but I have a child on the way and three sisters-in-law. My house looks like Tara from *Gone with the Wind*. I have servants out the ass that still make me look around when they call me Mr. Douglas. Perhaps this is normal and we're just used to not normal." They both laughed. "I'll keep you informed. Oh, and before I forget, Truman was hurt on his way home. I have no idea if he had any identification on him at the time to show where he worked, but I'd keep an eye out. You have a picture of the thug, right? I emailed it to you from the surveillance cameras that were running."

"I do. And I'll spread it around so that everyone here knows as well. I don't want to freak out Mercedes by talking to her through our link, but if you have given her a cell, I would like the number." Mason gave it to him. "Good. And for now, I'm going to see if Bonnie wants to come here. I think she'll be better off here than at home with her grandda. Maybe he'd like to come in for a bit too. Don't you think?"

"Yes. Good idea. I have to come into town in a bit, so I'll talk to her mom and see if they'll come in with me. That way I can drop them off with you. Are you sure you can handle a ten-year-old and Rose today?" Darin had no idea, but he wanted her with him. "All right then, I'll see you in about an hour."

He called Mercedes and told her that he needed her to stay close to the barns today. When she didn't even ask him why, he knew that someone had told her about what happened. He then told her that he was going to have Mason bring Bonnie in for him to keep an eye on.

"You don't have to do that. I know that you're busy and all." He said that he wanted to. "But she'll get in your way. At least here I can make sure that she's...."

"She'll be safe with me too. I promise you." When she didn't say anything, he asked her how she was feeling. "I kind of left you in a hurry. But Jessie said that he needed me right away."

"I understand. I'm just glad that you put me in my bedroom instead of leaving me on the floor like that. I don't know what I would have done if someone would have found me." He wanted to see her face, he knew it was red. "I have never wanted a man like I did you. Like I do you. It was...it was too much and not enough. Do you understand?"

"Yes, I do. And I want you as well. If you were here right now, I'd have you spread out on my desk naked and I'd be eating you." Her arousal hit him like a bat. "Christ, I can feel you. I wish I could smell you too."

"This is insane. What is it about you that makes me want to strip down and run to you?" He wanted that as well and thought of her naked running in the woods behind their house. "You make me want things that I've never thought of before."

"Like what? Naked in the woods? Would you like that? My big cat running after you, relying on your scent to find you before he eats your pussy too. He'd like that, Mercedes. To fuck you with his tongue as he drank you down." She moaned, and Darin had to adjust his cock or hurt badly. "How many times will you come for us? Your cream sliding down our throats until my cat lets me fuck you. I'd like to bend you over and fuck you hard from—"

"Stop." Her voice was dark, full of promise. "I have a sick donkey here and he's looking at me like I'm going to rape him. I won't, but this is just insane. You're making me insane with need."

"I'm right there with you, love." Her laughter came though the phone at him, and he smiled. "Just be careful around the ranches. And when you go somewhere, make sure that one of my brothers is with you. They will make sure that you're safe while I can't."

"He's really coming, isn't he? I mean, Nash is going to come here and make me go with him." Darin said he'd never get that far. "I don't want any of you hurt. Especially not you. But my daughter and father are my priority."

"As they should be. And when she gets here with me, I'll keep her as safe as you do. I really like her and she's fun." Mercedes told him it was because she wasn't around him all the time. "I'd like that too. For you to move into my house. It's safer for you both if you all do. Including your dad."

"I'll think about it." He told her he'd like that. "I have to go. Miss Donk is really not well, and I have to see to her.

There is a family coming out this afternoon and I need to get her a little better. I didn't know that handicapped children come out here to be with animals. That's the nicest thing I've ever been a part of."

"Several months ago this little boy came out with his family. Cortland Anderson is his dad. Cort was dying, and his wish was to ride a pony. When he died last month, it hurt all of us...Susie most of all. It's why she's called it the Anderson Foundation." Mercedes asked him how come it wasn't public. "Because it's not for the public to know about when the families just need some quiet time with their dying children. That's what Donk is there for."

"I think it's wonderful. And I'm going to do my best to take care of her for the children." He knew that she would. "And you keep an eye on my little girl. I'm trusting you with her."

"Thank you. You have no idea how good that makes me feel." After hanging up with her, he made his rounds.

Today was going to be a big day for them all. Jessie was calmer now that Julia had shown up with help. Darin called the hospital to check on Truman and was told he was doing well. An hour later, Bonnie showed up and he put her to work taking notes for him. By the time the Rose group showed up, Darin had fallen in love with the little girl as much as he had her mom. He had a family now.

~~~

Nash was nursing his arm when Rocky joined him in the waiting room. The doctor had been called to say Nash was coming in and he'd better be ready. Not only had he been ready for him and his men, but he'd cleared out his patients for them as well. He didn't want their germs and thought it cruel of them to think that he should have to endure their nastiness. Nash was fully prepared to kill them all, but this was better. For now, anyway.

"What did you find out?" The big man that they had cornered had done a number on him and his men. Nash had heard that he knew the Douglas people and he wanted him to give them answers. Had he not been there too, he might not have believed that a grown man would have been able to not just hurt his men but kill one of them. Rocky, too, was hurt, but he told Nash that he was going to be fine.

"He's got enough guards on him to make me think he wasn't your normal cook. Christ, I can't even get on the floor he's on without someone frisking me and telling me I need proper ID. Who the fuck was that monster?"

"I don't fucking know, but I think it's a good thing that Ben is dead. Or I'd be demanding the same answers from him as well." Ben had set it up to take the man and get answers. All they'd been able to get was their asses handed to them. "Please tell me they don't think the fucker is going to make it. I don't want him hanging around right now. I have to get the wife."

"I have no idea, but I'd say he's a damn sight better than Ben is right now. We can't even go in and claim his fucking body. That shithead, he's one tough motherfucker." Figures, Nash thought. Of course he was going to be just fine, while Nash was sitting there with what was more than likely a broken arm. "I did get some information on the place that he works. It's not going to be any easier to get in there than it was the hospital."

"Who the fuck are these people? When that bitch told me that Mer was coming here, she never said it was some sort of fortress. Mother fuck, I hate these people." For a week now he'd been trying to gather some information that would get him in and out with his wife. But at every turn there was someone telling him he'd be better off to forget her if she was with the Douglas family. Fuck that shit. Whoever these people were, they were going to die as surely as he was sitting there. Even if he had to do it himself.

"They got money too. And I mean a lot of it. The mayor is related to one of the Douglas men, married to some rancher. I bet that is a great bedtime story. Anyway, she's like worth billions. And yeah, I said billions. Her parents live with them. And the White House might be easier to breach than that house. They have fences along the fences there. And the staff is as loyal to them as I am to you." Nash was called back to have his x-rays read to him. Rocky came with him to finish with his information. "There is another one that is married to some broad that owns like most of the town. Snow. Her daddy has big bucks too, and has built them a house that is fucking huge and just as hard to get into. I tell you, it's like they knew you were coming and they set out to piss us off at every turn."

Nash wasn't getting any happier with this shit. Every time before this, he'd had her begging him to not hurt her within an hour. Now she'd not only left the area that he had people watching her in, but she'd come all the way across the States and hidden from him again. When he found her, and there was no doubt that he would, he was going to make her pay for every little thing that he'd had to go through to get her ass back where it belonged.

"They found Jacks, by the way. His body was reported sometime this morning, so she's more than likely heard about it." Well fuck, Nash thought, that wasn't going to help him either. "And that woman, Sanders from the clinic. The police had been holding her name for next of kin, but I guess they found them. They're saying some sadistic fuck killed her."

"Well, that's good news. I'd really hate to think no one noticed me." Rocky and he laughed, and Renshaw came in the room. "Well? Am I gonna have to wear a cast? I'm telling you right now, I don't have time for this shit."

"It's not broken. Badly bruised but not broken." That couldn't be right, and he said so. "I've gone over the x-rays myself three times. No breaks. But you're lucky. That guy that came in before you, he's going to be out for a long time. Whoever broke his leg, they did a bang-up job of it. Seventeen breaks in his tibia alone. And his fibula is going to need to be reinforced with steel rods before he can ever hope to walk again."

"So? He knows that working for me has some fall backs. And don't even bother sending me the bill. He got the shit knocked out of him on his own." Renshaw said nothing but asked if he wanted it wrapped or did he want to have a soft cast on it. "I want it fucking healed now, not to wait around for a couple of weeks."

"Six. Maybe longer. I have no way of knowing without the proper equipment." Nash reached for his gun but before he could use it, Renshaw spoke again. "You kill me and everyone will know who did it. I've taken pictures of you and have them waiting to be sent out should I meet with an untimely death."

Nash shot him in the head. "Don't you know that you don't threaten a man with a picture when he has a gun pointed at you? Moron." He looked at Rocky. "Find out who he might have sent it to. Not that it matters. Once I have Mer back where she belongs, no one is going to touch me. Not and live to tell about it."

Rocky nodded and picked up the rubbery gauze that was on the tray. As he started to wrap Nash's arm up, Rocky told him about the rest of the Douglas family. Nash thought he was going to enjoy killing them. And when he found Mer, he was going to kill that fucking brat of hers too while she watched him.

Dealing in drugs the way he had, among other things, Nash had a pretty good understanding of the shit that was in the office. Taking what he thought might help him with the pain, he had Rocky torch the place. The body would still be found, but it would take them longer to not only figure out who it was but also how he'd been killed. Nash had a feeling that time was running out for them to get in and out of this town. There were just too many good guys waiting around to try and take him out. And those Douglas people were going to wish they'd never heard of Mer Crosby. He certainly did.

"Why do you want her so much? I mean, really? What is she but a woman that hates you as much as you do her?" Nash had just popped several of the pain killers or he might have been pissed enough to hit Rocky. If nothing else, tell him to fuck off. "I mean, you've had other women that left you. Even a wife or two. Why haven't you just killed her off and been done with her?"

"She thinks she's better than me. And even with a fucking gun to her head she said no to me. It wasn't until I had it pointed at her daddy did she say yes when she was supposed to. And she lied to me." Rocky said all women lie. "Yes, but this was when she said she'd love, honor, and obey me."

"Seriously? That's it? You're going to hold her to a promise that you made her give you with a gun to her head? That's fucked up, Nash, even for you." Nash smiled. "Really? What are you doing with her?"

"It is, isn't it? And anything I fucking want. She belongs to me until I say differently." He was beginning to mellow out and smiled. "Really, it's because despite the fact that I hurt her, dragged her through the mud and back, she never gave me what I wanted most. She never feared me. She might have been pissed about what I did to her, but she was never really fearful of me. And that is what it's all about. I want to earn her fear."

"I'm pretty sure you scared the shit out of her when you tried to take the brat from her." The drugs were giving him a nice buzz now, and he wanted to enjoy that in silence. But Rocky wasn't quitting. "Nash, what are you going to do to her when you get her this time? I hope you know that she's not going to be easy unless you kill that kid."

"I'm going to. While she watches. And when the brat is dead and cold, I'm going to kill Mer. But not quickly. I want her to know just what sort of monster she was married to." Rocky said he was pretty sure she knew that. "Yes, but I want her to say it back to me. Tell me that I'm a fucking monster. I want to hear it from her own lips."

He let the good buzz from the drugs take him under. Nash wasn't worried that he was in a car without his gun. There was a good chance that he'd not be able to lift it up even if he were to be under attack. But he knew that Rocky would make sure that he was safe. And that was what he liked the best about the man. He was loyal and reliable. Things he didn't ever get from women.

When he woke, he was in a bed. Nash looked at the soft cast on his arm and smiled. Rocky was going to get a bonus for this trip. The man had gone above and beyond his normal duties. As Nash lay there thinking about the fucking bitch of a wife, something else occurred to him that he'd forgotten to put on his list. She'd lied to him about her daddy.

He remembered her telling him that he'd died of a heart attack before the brat had been born. He had slapped her that day, knocked her to the floor. And when she didn't even shed a tear for what he'd done to her, he asked her where Daddy dearest was.

"I told you, he died." She might have, he remembered thinking. But since he rarely if ever listened to her, he hadn't known. "He's been gone for three months."

"Well, that really is too bad, now isn't it? I guess that I'll have to think of something else to hold over your head." He looked at her belly, just beginning to show. "That'll do nicely. And the first time that you get out of line, I'm going to put that thing in the oven and have you eat it when it's done."

"You're a sick fuck." He'd hit her then, hard enough to knock her out and to bloody her mouth and nose. It had always bothered him that no matter what he did to her, that brat stayed planted where it was.

It was something he'd been really pissed about too. When he'd knocked her down the stairs once, she was able to keep it all snug in her. Nash had often wondered if it knew that it was short for this life and had clung to her mother's pussy like a lifeline.

He'd never gotten the baby alone, and the one time that he'd tried to take it from Mer, she'd cut him with a knife. He'd had nineteen stitches and she'd gotten the police involved. That was when she'd filed for and was granted a divorce. The judge had not granted one of those again. Nash knew that for a fact. Killing him had been a great pleasure for him.

Nash called Rocky and had him come to his room. When he got there, Nash had a plan. It was time to end this thing once and for all.

"Find me one of the others, those Douglas men or one of the wives. I don't give a shit who. I want them here tonight.

If she wants to involve them, then by all means let's give her what she wants." Rocky asked him if he meant the brat. "No, she won't last as long as I want one of the others too. When she comes here, and she by God will, I want her to be entertained by this as much as I'm going to be."

"I can do that. You need a place that's quiet, or do you really want this person here?" He thought about that too and looked around the room he was in. "The man that owned this house, someone is going to miss him soon enough, don't you think? Maybe we should think about getting us fresh digs. Something a little off the beaten path."

"You're right. Find me a nice quiet building with a sublevel. I have a need to make someone scream. And a great deal." As he finished dressing, he thought of something else. This might be the best time he'd ever had fucking his wife over. At least he didn't have to get his dick dirty this time. "And look for a house that we can spread out in too. I want you closer now that this thing is coming to a head. And money...I want you to see about getting me some ready cash too. About a hundred thousand should be good."

"Will do. I might need time on the money. Just so you know, I have to find a place to send it to." Nash told him that was fine. "All right. I'll see you in a bit."

Nash was ready. Mer was going to come here. He was going to make her suffer, and when he was done, he was going to kill her. He even had a new wife all lined up to take her place.

CHAPTER 7

The house was beautiful. Moving from room to room, all she could think about was this was hers. Darin had asked her to have a look around it before he got home so that if there was anything that she thought they might need, he could get it. She wondered if there was a more fully stocked house than this one. Even the pantry was stuffed full. Bonnie came into the kitchen with her and looked shocked.

"What is it? Is there someone here? Come to me." She shook her head and smiled. "Bonnie, you're scaring Mommy right now."

"I found my room." She said it reverently, like not only had she found the room she wanted, but that it was perfect in every way. "You said we were going to stay here. Right? If we do, I'm going to ask Darin if I can have that room. It's not girly at all."

"Well, let me see it. And so you know, we're not sure about staying here. I mean, we might have to run away again." The look on her daughter's face crushed her. Taking her into her arms when she stared up at her, Mercedes cried too. "I'm sorry, baby. I really am, but we don't want these people to get hurt because of my ex-husband, do we?"

Mercedes had never referred to Nash as Bonnie's dad. Not that she didn't know who he was, but there was a burden there, one that she tried not to attach to Bonnie if she didn't have to. Nash Crosby was a fucking bastard, and she wished now that she'd killed him rather than just divorced him.

"He's a monster." She couldn't disagree with Bonnie, so she didn't. "But I don't think that we're going to have to leave here, ever. Darin and his brothers are going to take very good care of us. Even Mr. Landon said he'd do anything in the world for us to be able to stay here. He has a gun in his boots all the time, did you know that?"

"No, I didn't. But it's not very fair of us to bring our problems to our new friends." Her daughter looked so crestfallen that Mercedes felt badly. "Show me this room you want to sleep in. And I guess there's a pool too. Maybe this summer we can get you some lessons. But first we have to see about this school. Julia said it's really nice."

The room was exactly what she might have gotten Bonnie had she had the funds. There were posters on the wall of horses in races. Steeple jumps and other activities. Even the bedspread, one made just for a little girl, had ponies all over it and even a pony-shaped pillow. Boxes were set around the room, most of them empty of anything, but some had books in them, trophies as well that had Mr. Landon's name on them, as well as Emma's. As they were marveling over it all, there was a knock at the front door and they both went to answer it.

"My lady." She didn't know the man and backed from him when he bowed before her. "I am the cook, missus. Benson Fox. I usually go by simply Fox. I have worked in this household before, and have been asked to come in and help out."

"I don't know you." He nodded and handed her a phone. "Who am I talking to? And why do I need a cook?"

"Hello?" The voice sounded like Katie McBride, but Mercedes wasn't sure until she spoke again. "I'm so sorry, Mercedes, but I meant to tell you about Fox before now. He used to cook for us when...well, before. When we moved in with Emma and Mason he just hung around waiting for someone to beg him to come cook for them. He's a doll and we love him to pieces. He wants to cook for you and your family."

"I wasn't aware that we'd need a cook." She invited the man in, and he went to the kitchen with Bonnie. They were talking about cookies and such when she realized that Katie was talking.

"You have a huge family, child. Over two dozen of them now if you count Landon and I. Oh, and I so hope that you count us. But as I was saying, Fox doesn't just cook. He runs the place too. I don't know what I would have done without him most days. I'm telling you the man is a wizard at all he does. Laundry too, if you can believe it." Mercedes started to ask again if she'd need a cook or even one that did laundry, but Katie seemed to be on a roll and she wasn't slowing down. "He's got training as a physical therapist as well. We thought it would be wonderful for your dad. As will the pool. Did I mention there is a lift for someone that is handicapped? It's in the pool house."

"There's a pool house?" She went to the back of the house and got her first look at the pool, and the house that was set back from it. "This place is huge. I mean, how many bedrooms are there? I would like to talk to you about the little girl's room too. I noticed that there are boxes there, as well as some personal things."

"I'll talk to Emma. But to be honest with you, child, I don't think she'll want any of it. We were in the process of packing her younger version up when...when things happened." Mercedes had heard about their son and what had happened to him. "The room was left that way when she moved out to go to college. I suppose we should have packed things up before then, but instead of growing out of the room, she moved to another one in the household. And to answer your question, there are seven bedrooms, not counting the master. Five full baths and a couple of half ones. We had planned on a large family when we built, and things just didn't work out for us."

"I'm sorry." She told her it was fine. "Bonnie really does like the room the way it is. And if there is anything in it that Emma wants back, I'm sure she'd understand." Katie said she'd speak to her today, but to think of them as her daughter's things.

"About Fox. If you'd be so kind to keep him on, Landon and I would appreciate it. I think he's bored, to be honest with you. And his salary is paid too." Mercedes started to protest but was cut off by Katie. Mercedes wondered at that moment why Darin thought her to be very easy going. The woman was very used to getting her way as much as Landon was. "I insist that we pay it. The reason the poor man is out of work is because we've not been able to return to that house. Too many memories, and not all of them good."

"I'll have to talk to Darin. It's his home." The silence at the other end had her nervous. "It is his home, isn't it? I mean, that's the impression he gave me."

"Oh yes, the home belongs to him. But to you as well. I thought you knew that." She asked her why she'd know that. "Well, child, you are his mate. Those Douglas men take care of their other halves. I do believe that he put your name on the deed as well. I mean, I can check for you, but I'm sure of it. Also on the deed to the Douglas House."

"I don't want him to do that." Katie said she was sorry to have upset her. "No, it's not that. But what if this doesn't work out? What if…? I don't know. What if someone else comes along that had no prior attachments to them or something?"

"Mercedes, it doesn't work that way with shifters. I'm not even sure that there are shifters out there like the Douglas men." Mercedes said she didn't think so either. "They're loyal, loving, and wonderfully good men. No one in the world would have done for us as they did. Sticking by us…I don't know if you know the entire story about my son or not, but he was a monster. He nearly killed my Landon. And he…and he…."

The sobbing broke her heart, and Mercedes kept telling her how sorry she was while the older woman cried. "I didn't mean to upset you. I'm so terribly sorry about that."

"No, no. It comes over me at times. My son was a terrible person. I've been seeing someone that has been helping me work through some of my sadness. It's been difficult to think of our little boy like he was." Mercedes told her again that she was sorry. "You have no reason to be. I'm…Landon and I are so happy to have someone in that house that has family…that will make the house a home again. I wasn't sure that I'd have ever been able to set foot in it again, but I might now. You'll make it yours, and I'll be able to think of happiness there again."

By the time they hung up, Mercedes was feeling a little overwhelmed again. She went in search of Bonnie and found her in the kitchen having a grilled cheese sandwich while Fox was making bread. Bread of all things. She asked him what he wanted to do.

"Do, my lady? I wish to run your home for you. Keep you and the master of the house safe, and this little one. I'm to understand that your father is to come here to live as well. I've had some experience in therapy that might help him along. He is bound to the chair. Am I correct?"

"Yes. When I was younger, he fell down the stairs of our home. He wasn't hurt, we didn't think, until later when his back started to hurt him. They found the broken disk too late. It had already done some nerve damage." She smiled when she thought of her father here. "I think he'll like staying here too. Katie said there was a pool sling for him to use as well."

"Yes. It was used when Landon fell from his horse one summer. He was determined to swim daily. I think it was what made him heal so quickly." He kneaded the bread dough a little longer and then smiled at Bonnie when she asked him what they were having for dinner. "I was thinking that tonight, as I am getting a late start on things, we'd have steaks on the grill and baked potatoes with homemade rolls. For dessert, you can pick."

The two of them talked about that, and Mercedes moved out to look over the rest of the house. It was going to take her forever to get used to something this big. And she was amazed at how comfortable she was here already. And with Fox. She felt as if she'd known him her entire life.

~~~

Rose seemed to be enjoying himself. Several of his staff came in a little early, and Darin had worked with Julia in getting them a table set for the six of them. By the time they were finished eating and everyone was in some of the other rooms, Darin felt as if he'd been run over a couple of times then set back up on a shelf to be in pain. He looked up when his door opened and Zach walked in and sat down across from him.

"I want you to know, first of all, if I find this fucker, he's going to be a dead man where he stands. Secondly, if you want first dibs, then you're going to be out of luck. He has a list of people after his ass that will make Dirk look saintly." Darin asked him if he was talking about Nash Crosby. "Yes. Holy shit, Darin. Your mate? She's been put through some hell with this guy."

He took the file from his brother and was looking it over when Zach made his way to the conference table that had some desserts on it from Julia. She had brought them to him earlier and was wondering if any of them would suit for him, and so far there hadn't been anything that he didn't like. Zach asked if he could have some.

"Sure. But whatever you eat, you have to give an opinion on. Write what you think of it on the paper next to each thing. If you don't, she'll have my head." Zach moaned when he bit into one of them. "Is that the strawberry crunch? I told her I'd have those at every meal if she had them here."

"This orange thing is awesome. Is that blueberries? Holy shit, those are almond bars too. Do you suppose if I gave her an order, she'd make these for me to take home? Christ, this is some good stuff." His plate was full by the time he came back to the chair. "I'd weigh six hundred tons if I had to be a taste tester here."

"I know. Earlier she brought me slices of bread. Rose was in here, and he nearly had a fit when she told him that was it when he finished off two loaves of them. She promised him she'd have some for dinner tomorrow for him. I swear, I think we've hit on a gold mine here with her. I mean Truman can cook, but she can bake circles around him when it comes to pastries and breads." Zach was stuffing more in his mouth as Darin went over the file. "How many times do you suppose she was hurt that didn't require her going to the hospital?"

"More than we want to think about, I'm thinking. There was one time that she was hurt so badly that she missed a week of work. I don't have a report on it, but the docs that she worked with said she'd often come in to work with bruises on her." He asked her about Milly. "I think that he was hurting her as well and that she wasn't a willing snoop for him. But she did it to keep from being hurt. She was the only one feeding him information as far as I can tell. Most of those other doctors had no idea that Mercedes even had a kid, much less had been married. They knew that she was having man issues as one of them said, but they didn't inquire. One of them told me that they were glad she worked there because she never said no when they asked her to take a weekend. Oh, and she was never going to make partner. They liked having her where she was."

"What a piece of shit." Zach agreed and went back for seconds and thirds. "You're going to tell Mom why you can't eat dinner."

"Grow up." Darin laughed and looked down at some of the reports that Zach had found for him. "Oh, before I forget, there was some money in her account. I had Ed move it to your account. Also, there is an insurance policy that has never been cashed that was her mom's. I'm not sure why, but I had Ed look into that as well. He said that there is no limitation on it, so if her dad turned it in now, the only difference would be there would be more interest on the money. I don't know how much it was worth, but Ed said he'd look."

There were sixty-one reports on Mercedes with injuries. Not all of them required stitches or even x-rays, but that was no less painful for him to read. As he read the more recent of the thick file, he noticed something else. Nash was using knives as well as his fists on her. He asked Zach about it.

"I saw that too. And if you look at some of them that happened within the last few weeks prior to her coming here, you'll see that someone else is helping him out. There's a lefty in the picture." He asked him how he knew that. "I'm brilliant? Nah, one of the doctors at the hospital where she was being treated told me. He said something about the angle of the cuts on her."

Zach was still eating when Julia came for the platters. He went over each one with her, telling her why he liked certain ones over the others. His favorite was the same as Darin's, the strawberry crunch. When she left them with the promise of more treats tomorrow, Darin closed the file.

"She's at the house now. I hope she likes it as much as I do." Zach said that she needed a car. "Mason made sure she had one for the time being. But she's under the assumption that it's just for work. I have no idea, as I've not had time to talk to Mason about it. But I can't afford a new car right now. My truck barely starts on most mornings, guzzles gas like it's free, and has four tires that are only the idea of being made of rubber. We need to win the lottery or something."

"I have money. I mean, I can lend you some if you want." He thanked his brother but declined. "I had some pretty good luck the other night. I bought a bunch of lotto tickets and a few of them paid off. I do that sometimes."

"You do. Found money, you call it." Zach nodded. "I've been putting my extra cash in a jar in my...our bathroom. There's not much in it, couple hundred bucks. But I think I'm going to need it to pay for Bonnie's uniforms and stuff."

"Let me help you. I swear to you, I did really well." Darin laughed and asked him how well he'd done. "I won two different tickets at ten grand each. And three more that were over five hundred dollars each."

"Holy shit, Zach, that's great." Zach nodded, his face a little red. "You should buy yourself something nice with it. That's enough to put down on a nice house."

"I thought about it, really I did, but...I was actually thinking along those lines and decided that it's just too much. You remember the house down the street from ours when we were growing up? Someone bought it a few years ago and started to renovate it. I'm not sure what happened, but they sort of stopped about halfway into the interior and now the bank owns it. I was thinking of seeing if I could buy it cheap and fix it up." Darin told him that was an excellent idea. "Yeah, I talked to Landon and Palmer about it. Not to borrow money but because if I ask any of the others about it, they'd buy it for me and then have it fixed up. I want to do this on my own."

"I don't blame you. My house is...I'm lucky in that. Especially now that I have a ready-made family." Zach handed him a sheet of paper. "What's this?"

"The specs and the asking price. Landon is going to go with me in an hour to check on it with the bank. He promised not to pay for it but to help me with the paperwork. They're asking too much for it, he said." The asking price was over a hundred grand, well over what a partial house should have been. "There's something that I didn't know when I started this thing. Look at the amount of acres on the property."

"Seven hundred? Wow, I had no idea. Maybe that is a good price." Zach said he thought so too now. "Ah, so you thought that if you couldn't afford the house, you'd just spend your money by lending it to me? If Landon wants to help you with the purchase price, Zach, you'd not be sorry.

He's a good and fair man, and this is really a good deal. I know you want to do this on your own, but that'll help you."

"Yeah, I was kinda hoping you'd tell me that I should think of another property." Darin asked him why. "Because it's going to be expensive. It's a lot of land that I don't even know what I'm going to do with. It's farmland, or it was once. I actually thought of growing hay on it and some other grain to sell to the farms here. But Christ, that's a huge amount on speculation."

"I know how much Susie and Gerard spend on hay a week, and if you could make it work, I'm sure they'd rather pay it to you. And Mason buys alfalfa for the cattle he has, so I know that you'd have a built-in customer there." Darin watched his brother; seeing him struggle like this made him glad that he'd come to him. "You're being paid by the ranches now, right? I mean, you're making pretty good money."

"Yes. I even have managed to pay up on all my own bills and put some away. Not counting the lotto winnings." He grinned. "I'm going to confess something to you. I have a lot more than the twenty grand that I won from the tickets. I think I have this Zen-like thing going on. I have closer to fifty. Lately it's like I can't pick a bad ticket."

"Christ, that's wonderful. Fifty grand will go a long way to making this work for you. I'm guessing that you want to keep most of that back to use as seed money?" Aunt Georgie had always told them, save your seeds for a nice planting. It wasn't until they started making money recently that he understood how that worked. "The house? Is it in good enough shape to live in while you work on it?"

"I think so, but I'm not so sure that everyone will agree with me. There is power in it, running water and all, but no hot water and there is very little in the way of grass. Mostly it's mud. But the good news is that the roof is in great shape, the flooring has been reinforced, and all the plumbing and electrical stuff has been replaced and updated. No furnace or other household things like a sink or fridge." Zach laughed. "You might say that I'm living in a very nicely put together box with power."

As they made plans to go over to the house soon and have a look, Landon showed up. The man was almost giddy to be helping Zach, and he'd already gone over to the house before coming here. When he pulled out his phone to show them pictures, Darin could see that the man wanted to buy it for Zach and then help him out with the house and land.

"Talked to the banker too. Nice man, but he's a stickler for rules. Don't know if that works all the time, but in this one, I'm thinking you won't get a good deal." Zach started to stand, his hand out, thanking Landon for his help. "Now hold your horses a bit there, boy. I didn't say it wasn't doable, just not through the bank. I'll lend you the money. And hear me out before you start shaking that head like it's got a crick in it or something."

"I really wanted to do this on my own. You know, I'm young, stupid, and have nothing better to do with my time than to work a farm I have no idea if I can work or not." Darin could see how painful this was for his brother, but Landon laughed.

"You're a lot like your momma. Anyone ever tell you that? Can see her sitting right there where you are and telling me that it's her job or something, and that I should butt out. Lovely woman, your momma was, but she'd tell you to do this. If for no other reason than I'm a good man." Zach looked at him, then back at Landon. "You know I'm an honest man."

"Of course I do. We all do. But like I was saying—"

"That banker is gonna charge you an interest rate that will pull you under. He's right in it...you have no collateral, not much in the way of money, and you got a job that depends on your brothers. I know that you can make it work because I know you. He doesn't. I'll lend you the money at less than half the rate he would. There won't be any fees or anything that you don't know up front. Oh, and I done talked to him there. He's gonna let me take it off his hands for sixty-seven thousand. That's a mite less than we thought. The man was glad to have it gone off his books."

"You bought it. What will you sell it to me for?" Landon told him what he paid for it, sixty-seven. "You'll sell it to me for less than you paid for it and at a lower interest rate on top of that. What do you get out of this?"

"Nothing. I really...have I told you what it's like for me not to have to go out and worry over the ranch anymore? Not that I did much worrying anyway, but I did feel like I had to go out and see to things. Since your brother took over we've already made a bigger profit this year than we did the last five total. He's a good man." Darin wasn't sure were this was going, but waited on Landon to continue. "Since he's been working the ranch, I've invested in a girly catalog, worked out the plans to have a homeless shelter put in, with the help of your brother Jace. Got me a soup and salad kitchen going in to supplement them out-of-towners that sister of yours is bringing in, and we've made some little bitty plans on putting in a second gas station. One that will feed them big trucks when they come in. Diesel. I've been talking to some of the downtowners, and we've decided that we wanna make the town come back. And I think we will. But I'm bored if you want to know the truth. Helping you boys is...well, it's like I'm helping family. And you are my family."

"I don't know what to say." Landon told him to say yes. "Yes. I... yes, I'll let you sell me the ranch. But I'm telling you right now that I'm going to need more than just this kind of help. I'm thinking of becoming a farmer, too."

"Holy shit, boy. Why would you want to go and do a fool thing like that?" Landon wasn't mad, and Darin could tell that Landon liked the idea. His mind was already working on a tractor for Zach, he'd just bet.

CHAPTER 8

The offices were perfect, and she had a long list of things to get done today before her day was even to begin. But all she could think about was making love to Darin all night last night. He'd been so romantic and so loving. Darin had made her cry, it had been so amazing.

When he got home, he brought his brother Zach and a dozen roses for her. Zach, it seemed, had wanted to take Bonnie to his house with his aunt to watch movies and have pizza. Bonnie had been so excited to go that she had to come back to the house twice to hug her. Darin had planned well, it seemed.

"This will work out really well. I wanted to go over some of the changes we might need to make in the house. And before I forget, Emma told Bonnie she could have all the things in her old room so long as she took care of them. I don't think that'll be a—"

The kiss took her breath away. In mid-sentence he pulled her body to his and kissed her like he'd been holding onto it all day. Holding onto his shoulders, she buried her nose into his neck. Then he picked her up in his arms and started toward the master bedroom she'd seen earlier. The man held her in his arms like she was so precious to him.

After standing her on her feet, he proceeded to take her clothing off. Not in a hurried way, but slowly and reverently, kissing her flesh as he exposed it. Touching her too, just a brush of his fingers here, then a gentle touch there. When he had her blouse unbuttoned, he didn't remove it but left it hanging on her as he made his way to her pants, socks, and shoes. Standing before him in just her blouse and bra pantie set, she felt loved, worshipped even, as he stood watching her.

"Do you have any idea what I think of when I see you this way?" She knew in her heart that he wasn't talking about sex, but of something more. "Love. This is, in my heart, what love is like. I don't think there are words out there to tell you or anyone how I feel about you. It's more than just love. It's everything to me. Seeing you standing here exposed to me shows me that no matter what, you love and trust me."

"I do. I didn't know that until just now, but I do love you, Darin." He nodded and touched his finger to the area that her blouse didn't cover. "I want you to take me. I want to feel you inside of me. I need to touch you like you have me."

"My cat wants to taste you as well." Her body warmed. The thought of his great cat touching her with his mouth made her wet, heated, and swollen for him. "He can smell you. We both can. The way your pussy is ready for him. When he drinks from you, he'll bring you quicker than I will be able to and drink you down."

"Yes." Almost as soon as the word left her mouth, his cat took him. Mercedes felt a little nervous. He was so large, his body much bigger than she'd realized. "I'm a little afraid of him. I know that he won't hurt me, but he's bigger than I am in some ways."

He will never hurt you. Nodding, she stood there. He'd told her about how they could speak like this earlier that morning. *He wants you. Take off your clothes for him and he'll show you how much.*

Her blouse came off first. She dropped it to the floor, letting it slide from her fingers as she watched his cat. Then her bra. It was new, lacy, and sexy, but she knew that for now the big cat was only wanting one thing from her. Pulling on the strings at the sides of her panties, she let the silk fall slowly, hiding herself until the last minute. As soon as she was naked, Darin's cat lunged at her and licked her clit with his rough, hard tongue.

"Darin." Mercedes hadn't been able to speak much more than his name around the emotions, all of them tight within her. She held the big cat, more to stand steady than to keep him there. But oh the things he'd done to her, the way he kept her coming over and over. Then he lifted his head, and she realized how weak he'd made her.

Go to the bed and lie down. She did so on wobbly legs and closed her legs tightly when his head sat on her knees. *He can feel your need, Mercedes. The same as I can. Let him have you. Then I can take you too.*

Opening her legs for him, she lay back on the bed. His tongue swiped over her thigh first, then into her pussy. Mercedes hadn't known what to expect to have him like this, but his tongue was thicker than Darin's, longer too. As soon as he fucked her with his tongue, she came four times in a row while he drank from her.

Every time she came, Mercedes was sure it was going to be her last. But the more he took her over the edge, the more the cat gave her. And when she screamed out her release once again, she felt the magic in the room and looked down her body to see Darin there. He lowered his head to her pussy slowly, never taking his eyes from hers.

"Mercedes?" It took her several seconds to bring herself from her memories and realize that the woman in front of her was someone she knew. When Susie laughed, Mercedes felt her entire body heat from embarrassment. "Yeah, they can make you forget that you're out in public, can't they?"

"I don't know what to…. He's like this…." Her face heated more. "I was thinking about him and got lost in it. Do you ever do that?"

"All the time." Susie sat on the chair that she'd only just put together. "I wanted to talk to you about something. We have two children coming out today that are going to need some special care. You don't have to do anything with them, but I wanted to give you a heads up that they'll be here. We usually only bring them out one at a time, but Bobby only has a few weeks to live and he wanted to come to the farm."

"I heard that you did this. I think it's the most wonderful thing in the world that you do this for so many children and their families. Some of these children, they'd never get the chance to see a real horse if not for you." Susie said nothing but watched the doorway. "When are they coming out?"

"Jack is on his way. Bobby is here now." Mercedes went to the doorway with her. "He's a lot worse than we were told. I don't think the parents want to see it yet."

"I don't know what I'd do if it were me." Susie said nothing. "What is it that he wants to do today? I mean, he must have a list of things he wants."

"He wants a pony ride. I'm not sure he's strong enough to make that work." They both watched as the young man struggled to hold his hand up to pet one of the gentler horses. Bride was there as well, watching them closely. "I think Bride knows that he's ill and wants to help him out. It's funny how animals have a sixth sense about things like that, don't you think?"

"Yes." Mercedes looked around her offices. "Susie, did you know that among the things that were sent here today that one of the things was a harness? A person to person one." Susie said she'd ordered it. "If Bride will let me, I'll ride with Bobby on the front of me. I'd say that you could do it, but I'm taller and might have an easier time of it."

Susie looked at her, then back at the boy and his family. Mercedes could see her mind working and wondered what she was going to say. When she told her to get the harness, Mercedes started to have second thoughts. What if the boy got hurt? Or the horse threw them both. Before she could voice these fears, Susie took off to the corral and to the big mustang.

The instructions were fairly easy to understand. She put it on first, then strapped the young man to her. The problem was, he was weak and heavier than she'd thought. It took both Mason and Landon to lift him to the saddle with her and then to buckle the harness around them both. Bride stood still for them as if he'd done this a million times before.

Mercedes had expected some objections from Bobby's parents, but they stood by, holding each other while their son was moved around to ready him for his first ride on a big horse. She knew that it hurt him. His cries of pain nearly had them all backing off. But he kept telling them to do this. He wanted to ride. As soon as Bride took his first walk around the fencing, she knew that this was the right thing to do. Bobby loved it.

"Again." She nodded as she moved around the circle again. Each time they got near some of the hands, all of them on the fence to watch, Bobby would wave at them. One of the men, she thought his name was Dick, took off his cowboy hat and handed it over to her. She put it on Bobby's head, to his great delight.

They made four trips around the yard. Each time she could feel him getting weaker, but he didn't want to stop. Finally, he told her when they were nearly halfway around the last time that he wanted her to stop. She did and waited for him to tell her to go again.

"I'm going to die. Today." She nodded. Mercedes knew that this was going to be his last day on earth the way he'd wanted this so badly. "My mom, she's going to be broken and I'm scared for her. Dad too, but he isn't always with me like my mom is. She's going to take this hard. But I'm really tired and need to just let go."

"She'll have today and your happiness that will bring her through. Don't you think?" He nodded, his head leaning heavily on her shoulder now. "You did this for her, didn't you?"

"Yes. My mom and dad have given up so much for me and I wanted to see them smile again." She knew on some level that he understood that they'd done it for him no matter what. "When I die, will you do me a favor? Will you call my mom and tell her that I loved her more than anything in this world? My dad too?"

"Yes. I'll do that, but they know that already, I think." He nodded and told her to go. As Bride started to walk around the fence again, she thought of something else. "Bobby, would you mind very much if I had a picture made of the two of us? I'd like to hang it in my office to remember you by."

"I'd like that very much." When they got to the men who were to help him down, they looked at her when they lifted him off the horse. Bobby was considerably weaker than he'd been before. With a small shake of her head, she got down off Bride and hugged Bride for what he'd done for them all today. The horse had given them both just what they had needed.

The picture was taken, and she told them that she enjoyed herself as much as he had. Dick told the young man to keep the hat, that he'd been thinking of getting himself a new one for a while now. Tears were filling everyone's eyes when he was lifted to the wheelchair and put in the back of the van. Bobby was going home today.

Mercedes worked the rest of the day on the opposite end of the ranch from Jack. It was not that she didn't care about him, but she wasn't sure her heart could have taken much more today. And when Bonnie came by after school, Mercedes hugged her a little tighter than she might have normally. By the time she'd seen her last horse and worked up his medical record, Mercedes felt drained.

~~~

Nash was pissed. Every time he spoke to one of the people in this town, each and every one of them had told him to shove off. One of them had even told him that he'd be fucking with the wrong people if he tried to get Mer back. He'd been ready to kill him too, when two people from the store came out and stood behind him. He looked over at Rocky when he cleared his throat.

"Do you think they know that you're here?" He looked over at Rocky and gave him a questioning look, as if to say, *really?* "I'm sure they know I'm here, but do you think they know you are as well? I mean, that could be a little bit of an issue for you should they find out. You're not supposed to be leaving the state and all."

"This is my wife we're talking about." Rocky didn't say anything about them being divorced. He'd done that before and had nearly been killed when Nash beat him to shit.

"When I have her, and I will, then I'll go back home and pretend that none of this ever happened. She should know better than to think she can get away from me, and I'm going to make sure she knows that it's over when I say it is. I know that it won't be long after we get back, but in that time, she's going to learn that what I say is law."

"She's not going to be coming back easy. You know that, don't you?" Nash said he was hoping she wouldn't. "Ah, you want her to fight you, do you? Well, that's all well and good for you, but I'm telling you right now, there are some big men on the property where she's supposed to be staying. And yesterday I thought for sure I was going to be killed by a pack of wolves. Motherfuckers knocked me down several times before I got off the property. And it was like they knew it, too."

"So you said. I doubt very much that the wolves, if that was even what they were, had any idea where the property lines ended. Perhaps you just tired them out running like a little girl." Rocky said nothing. "Speaking of which, have you had any luck getting that brat? I want her here so I can dangle her dead body in front of her mother. That'll be incentive enough to keep her in line, I think. And once the kid is dead, it'll be one less thing I have to be worrying over all the time. And that dad of hers too. But if you'd like, you can kill him wherever they have him hiding out. That motherfucker should have been dead long ago. Who the fuck wants a cripple in the house? I don't."

"She lied to you. I still can't believe that. The fucking bitch lied right to your face. Why do you think she thought that she could get away with that?" Nash said he was going to find out the answer to that as well. "Well, about the girl. I have a lead on her too. There's this school that she goes to that is really off the beaten path. I'm going to be there when she gets out tomorrow and take care of her. Well, I was gonna. Now I'll just bring her to you. We're gonna dart her and whoever is with her, and when they scramble like we know they will, we'll make our way in and nab her. She'll wake up about the time she's ready to be killed, I figure."

"See that you take care. I need to know that Mer knows that no matter what she does, I can find her and kill whatever she loves. I don't want her to love me, but she will mind what I tell her. When she said yes, no matter how I got her to say it, she knew damned good and well that I'm the one going to say that it's over. That bitch will pay for this. See if she doesn't." Nash wasn't sure yet how he was going to get her back home. He'd been about to book a plane for them all but knew that Mer would be an issue. "Did you have any luck getting some cash for me?"

"Yeah, but there was a glitch at the other end. Not sure what, but someone is looking into it. There is a place here that can receive money, but the most they'll take is five hundred at a time." Nash rolled his eyes. "That's what happens when you live in a small shit town, I guess."

After Rocky left him, Nash sat on the couch in the living room. The place wasn't bad, really, but it wasn't what he wanted in a home. Nash smiled when he thought of his home that no one but Rocky knew about. He'd been having some work done on it since he'd been out here too, and it was going to be perfect for keeping Mer in line.

Nash had more money than anyone realized. Millions and millions of dollars that he had stashed all over the place in his home. There were safes on every floor, hidden in walls and floors. He'd even hidden some of his ill-gotten gains in mattresses, under tile in the bathroom, and in the deep freeze in the garage. There was a substantial amount in a bank in

Switzerland, but that was his settling money. Money to be used to live off of when he was no longer welcome here.

He'd seen too many of his counterparts, other criminal types, that had been caught going to the bank for their escape money or travelling to some out of the way place to dig something up. He had money in a couple of banks. It wasn't all at his home. But sometimes, like today, he might need to have a little more than he'd brought, and this was how he'd get it. Nash prided himself on being prepared.

Even now he had enough money to buy and sell the little ranch operation that she worked for, he knew. A few ponies and a home was nothing to him, but he'd take it just to watch it burn if any of them fucked with him. Nash was almost hoping one of them would try and stop him from taking what was rightfully his. And Mer was fucking his. She had been since the first time he'd seen her.

Nash had seen her at a party. He'd not been invited, but it had been in the hotel he was having a meeting in and he had just joined the festive event. And what an event it had been. Food and drinks, people dancing and having a good time. And there she was, the center of it all, simply because she'd graduated from college. Like a woman needed a college education, he remembered thinking back then. But he could see that the people there had thought it a big deal. Nash had made his way over to her when she'd been talking to a group of people.

"Hello." She'd nodded her response and then turned her back on him. It was the first time in his life that he could remember someone doing that to him. When she continued to talk to the group in front of her, he calculated what it would take to get her to learn her place. The only thing he could think of was to slap the shit out of her. But he refrained. Barely. When she started to walk away from him, he grabbed her arm.

"Hey, what do you think you're doing? Don't you dare walk away from me. Just so you know, I think you're very rude. I wanted to talk to you." She had jerked her arm from his grip and backed away from him. "I said that I wanted to talk to you. Now don't be a cunt, and stand here and do as you're told."

"I have no idea who you think you are, and really, I don't give a shit, but I'm not some child to be ordered around. I think it's time that you left." This time when she turned her back on him, Nash saw red and jerked her around and slapped her. As soon as she hit the floor, her mouth bloodied, three men took him to the floor too. As they held him down, she was helped up and handed a washcloth.

"Toss his ass out. I don't know who he is, but I want him out of here." The men dragged and shoved him to the door of the hotel. When he was nearing the desk, he called for the clerk there to call the police. He wasn't going to be manhandled by a group of idiots. As soon as he was out of the building, he'd been surprised to see two uniforms there. He found out that they were there to congratulate Mer, but had arrested him and took him to jail instead. He'd started on his campaign then to have her brought to her knees.

He'd had both them officers killed the very moment that he'd been released. And the clerk from the hotel for not helping him out when she could have. Then Mer had disappeared for nearly a month before he'd been able to make her pay for her behavior. Marrying her had been a spur of the moment thing he'd regretted ever since.

Nash had never been able to kill her outright like she begged him to all the time. Not by her words really, but actions. It was as if she had a death wish or something, and he'd never been able to pull the trigger. Then she'd told him she was pregnant. It had taken him nearly the entire time of her body swelling like a fat pig to get her to tell him who the real father was. Nash did not want children and wouldn't believe that it had been his, no matter how many times she'd told him otherwise. It had taken him nearly his entire jail time to realize that she'd fucking lied to him when she'd told him a name. There had been no John Smith. In his anger, he'd not been able to see that and had lashed out at her again. Then the bitch had gotten a restraining order against him — fat lot of good that had done — and had been granted a divorce. Not that he'd let a little sheet of paper deter him from his plans. It hadn't stopped him from doing just what he wanted, when he wanted.

It had taken him little effort to ruin her after that. Charging up credit cards that he'd gotten in her name had been easy. With her being a vet of good standing, people had been falling all over themselves to give her ten to twenty grand a pop. He'd gotten a dozen or so cards filled out, charged them to the max, and had had a blast taking the shit to the dump. He didn't even care that it had been stolen, just so long as she didn't have it and had to pay for it. But the big car, the black SUV, had been the best. Christ, he'd even driven it around a little bit before leaving it running with the keys in it one day. He'd even had a plant in the bank to dip into her accounts when she had a couple hundred in it. Nash had figured that he had her just where he wanted her at all times. Then she'd run.

"Bitch will pay for that too." He was going to enjoy tearing her down. Just before he planned to kill her. And he would too. Of that, there was no doubt.

Not in money, no, that's not how she was going to pay, but with each punch to her face. Every time he had to cut into her. Every little thing he did to her was going to be one more thing he was going to mark off the list of shit she had done to him. As he'd been saying all along, she belonged to him, damn it. As he moved around the "borrowed" house, he thought of other things she was going to have to repay him for. This trip being one of them.

He'd had to get his hands dirty too, and that did not settle well with him. Nash never killed unless he had to, and even then he didn't enjoy it as much as Rocky did. Rocky, he'd come to figure out, was a sadist, which worked out well for them both as he took care of all the little problems that Nash didn't want to deal with. Which were mounting up since he'd been here taking care of his wife.

Smiling, he thought of the preparations that he'd made at his home. The little room he'd had put in for his dearly soon to be departed wife. He was pretty sure that she was going to die quickly, but he could hope that she'd last long enough that he felt justified in what he'd spent on the room.

There was a long table that he was planning to tie her to. Then there were the knives, all of them in varying lengths and steels that he was going to fuck her up with. There was even a bath he was going to bathe her in when he had had enough fun. No one would ever find even a hair of hers in his home when he sunk her body in the acid he'd purchased just for her. Nash wanted her alive, too, when he put her in it. He was looking forward to hearing her screams when she was dying.

He didn't get off on the sound of screams. Nor blood for that matter. Sometimes it even sickened him a little, all that red bleeding out of various places on a person's body. But for her, he'd suffer through it. To watch her while she suffered, the way she'd made him suffer, would be fulfilling to him. He might even let Rocky have some fun with her before bath time. He had a better stomach for it than he did anyway. Yes, it was going to be a good time to see Mer suffer at his hands.

When the phone rang, he picked it up and waited for Rocky to speak. He could hear other voices coming over the line, but he held it tightly to his ear to hear even a whispered sound should Rocky not be able to speak loudly.

"I get her today at the end of her school day. It's been arranged." The line went dead, and Nash sat there smiling. Today. This shit with that brat would bring it all to a head.

"Mer, my dear wife, you are going to pay for this shit. And I'm going to love every moment of it." Nash went to dress. He was going to establish an airtight alibi for today. Thinking of going out of town to a restaurant he'd heard about on the news yesterday, he was thinking of the new suit he'd gotten delivered just the day before. Nash was going to enjoy this, knowing that when he got back to the house, the brat would be there waiting for him.

CHAPTER 9

Bonnie hated riding in the big car to go home. The rest of the kids got to walk home, but she had to ride. She knew why, but that made it no less boring. No one made fun of her or anything. They were really nice, but she wanted to walk with them. Especially the boy named Patrick Sexton.

His daddy was the pack leader. And while he was a little older than she, he'd been hanging around her a lot since she'd started at her new school. Just yesterday he'd brought her a pretty bouquet of flowers and told her that they were from his momma's garden. She'd expected the other kids to tease her about that too, but they'd only nodded at her. Patrick was waiting for her at the limo when she came out of the school.

"I was going to go home with you today. My mom said that I can work over at the ranch with your mom to learn how to be a vet." She nodded, disappointed that her mom was going to be the one that he spent time with. "That way maybe I can stay for dinner and sit with you for a little while before I have to get back home."

"I'd like that. Fox is making lasagna tonight, and a salad." He nodded and told her that was fine. When he opened the door for her, she felt a sting in her arm and looked at the little arrow sticking out of her shoulder. "Patrick?"

Things were fuzzy then. Patrick was speaking to her, but they were both falling to the ground. Even before she could figure out that someone had shot them both with darts, she felt a tightening around her like someone had turned up all the power in the world. Then she realized what it was. Patrick had shifted and was standing over her as a big wolf.

She knew then that he'd been shot, this time with a real gun. There was blood on his shoulder dripping down on her face. She felt sickened that someone would do this to him. When he fell, his big body falling onto her, Bonnie thought he'd been killed. Then she screamed when someone grabbed her hair and started to pull her out from under him. That's when she saw the rest of the kids running back into the building, one of the teachers herding them like the cattle she'd seen on Uncle Mason's ranch. Her mind seemed to buzz out for a minute, thinking that whatever was going to happen, her mom was going to be very upset.

The man slapped her twice, and she opened her eyes to see who it was. Bonnie had no idea how long she'd been out, but when he slapped her a third time she tried to focus on what he was saying to her. Opening her mouth to try and tell him to shut up, her head hurt, she sat up when he was suddenly gone, his hand raking over her face as he disappeared. Bonnie felt sick to her stomach but looked for Patrick.

A wolf was tearing into the man that had tried to hurt her. Bonnie was really sick now, her belly churning and curling around until she leaned over to throw up. The man was screaming at the wolf, and Bonnie had a feeling that it was Patrick but wasn't sure. When the gun went off twice, she felt like someone had stabbed her in the chest. Lying back, she looked at the blood that was seeping through her shirt just as the wolf came back to her. Then he was Patrick.

"I've called the pack in." She nodded, not sure what he was talking about. "Stay with me, Bonnie. You can't die on me."

"I think I'm bleeding to death." Her voice hurt to hear. It was weak and she was getting dizzy from the pain in her chest. Looking down at herself again, she knew that this was bad. Her shirt was bright with her blood. "Patrick, I'm so glad that you were with me. I love you. Will you tell my mom and Darin that I love them too? And my grandda. I wish I could have known him better. Tell him I love him."

"You'll tell them." He looked up then and there was a bunch of wolves around them. "Dad, I can't let her die. She's my mate."

Bonnie thought of that word, mate. She'd heard it a lot over the last few weeks at the Douglas homes. Mate meant something, but her mind was fuzzing out again and she couldn't think. But when she opened her eyes again, not even realizing that she'd closed them, she saw the big wolf standing on one side of her and Patrick, as a wolf, standing on the other. They were so pretty, she thought. So big and gentle too.

"I don't want to die." He nodded and licked her face. "Please, I don't want to die. You have to do something."

I will, love. She nodded. *You're not going to make it unless I do this now. I know you have no idea what's happening, but it's the only way we can save you. I'm going to change you. I don't know if you'll survive or not, but you're dying now and I won't...and I can't let that happen.*

"Change me?" She faded out again and woke when the most incredible pain she'd ever had tore into her belly. They were eating her. The big wolf at her side was biting into her leg; Patrick was tearing into her belly. Bonnie screamed over and over for them to stop, but they didn't. The pain was incredible. Things flashed behind her eyes. Her body felt like it was being ripped apart. Her last thought was she was dying. Right there, she was going to die.

She knew that she'd never see her mommy again and let the darkness take her under.

~~~

Darin was working the ranch today. Jessie had told him that he could handle it with no one in the place until the next week, and Darin had wanted to get out of the office. The sun was shining, there wasn't a cloud in the sky, and he was about as happy as any man could be.

As he punched the posthole digger into the ground for the fourth time, he looked at Mason when he said his name. He and Logan had been at this for a while now and were glad for the help. Darin started to ask him if he'd come out to work when he looked at his face.

"There's been an accident." The posthole digger was gone from his hands, and Landon and Zach were holding him up. As he fell to the ground, all he could think about was Mercedes. "Bonnie's been hurt badly. She's at the pack house now. They tried to convert her to save her life."

There was more, he was sure of it, and that Mason had told him. But his mind was blank now. All he could think about was his daughter and that she was hurt. He looked up at Mason again.

"Mercedes?" He said that she was with Holly and Emma but didn't know anything yet. "Was it Nash? Did he do this?"

"We're working out the details. All I know for sure is that she and some of the other kids were coming out of the school when she and Patrick Sexton each took a dart. It didn't affect him much, but she fell to the ground. By the time he was able to shift and go after her, she'd been hit a few times. Patrick killed the man who had tried to take her, and the both of them were shot in the process. As I said, I don't know everything but that the man has been killed and that Bonnie was going to die if they didn't do something right then."

Darin found himself in a truck moving along the fields quickly. Every bump they hit seemed to jar another memory of the little girl that had come to mean so much to him front and center. He looked over at Logan when he told him that they were home.

Mercedes was in the corral with several horses when he got out of the truck. He had no idea what she saw when she turned to look at him, but she dropped everything in her hands and ran to him. He was sobbing as he told her what he'd found out. In minutes they were headed to the pack house and Mason was updating them on things.

"A man by the name of Rocky Bends shot the two of them. We know now that he worked for Nash, and that he and a couple of others with him shot darts at Patrick and Bonnie to bring them down. Bonnie took it hard and was out, but Patrick was able to shake most of it off. Thankfully. If he hadn't, then there is no telling how that would have ended." Mercedes said Rocky always had a couple of men with him. "Well, he's dead now, as are the other two that had been with him. Patrick and a pack of wolves killed them before they went to take care of Bonnie. So you know, Patrick told his dad that Bonnie was his mate. So, Darin, I'd tread carefully where she is concerned."

"What do you mean, she's his mate? She's ten years old." Mason didn't say anything to Mercedes. Her anger was palatable. "If he's hurt her, I will kill him. That's my baby girl, and I won't have her sold into slavery."

"Honey, he can't hurt her." Mercedes turned to him, and he could see the fire in her eyes. "You have to listen to me. He won't ever hurt her. He's more than likely saved her life."

"I don't care. He's not going to touch my little girl." Mason said nothing more as they drove to the house. Neither did Darin. She was on edge, and he knew that the slightest thing would set her off again. Mercedes was out of the car even before it came to a full stop. Darin was right behind her.

The pack looked as if they were crowded in the big bedroom. Paddy and his wife were nearest the door, but no one stopped Mercedes when she barged past them. Darin looked in the room and saw Patrick there, but he didn't go any closer to the bed and the small bundle there. His heart broke for her; his little girl had been hurt so badly. Paddy spoke quietly to him as Mercedes cried, holding Bonnie's hand.

"He had me help him. She was dying and we had no choice. You know that, don't you, Darin? We would never have done it if we'd had a choice in the matter." Darin nodded at Paddy and asked him how she was. "I think it worked for her. Her heart rate has picked up in the last ten minutes. Her skin isn't as cold as before. She's gonna be weak for a time, but we think she's going to make it. I know I keep saying this, but there wasn't any waiting around for permission on this. Darin, there would have been no waiting for an ambulance. She was bleeding out."

"I know that." He moved into the room, and Patrick stood up, his small body hard with terror. "You know what she is to me?"

"Yes, sir. But she's my mate." Mercedes slapped young Patrick, and Darin watched him struggle to keep his wolf under control. Darin thought that had it been anyone else than Bonnie's mom, he would have killed her. "I never meant for her to be hurt, Mrs. Douglas. She was dying."

"So you say. And now you expect me to just let you have her? Because you claim that she's your mate? I don't fucking think so. As soon as she's well enough to move, I'm taking her out of here and to a doctor. If you so much as —" Before Darin could move to calm her, Julia stood in front of Mercedes and handed her a bag. "What's this? A peace offering? I don't want anything from you but my child."

"Look at it. Look at it and tell me what you think happened out there today." Julia's wolf was there, just on the surface, and he'd bet anything she was ready to tear into his mate. If she did, then all hell would break loose.

Mercedes pulled the cloth from the bag and stumbled back from it after holding it up. Julia spoke again, this time her voice calmer, her body not as stiff. "She was as good as dead when he changed her. They were gonna take her with them, and had my son not taken a bullet then I'm...they tried to kill my baby too. Those men had shot her as if she was nothing to any of us. Just look at that blood, Mercedes. And where the bullet entered her chest. An inch to the right and she would have been gone. There would have been no saving her from that. I'm surprised she was able to tell him to tell you that she loved you and Darin."

The blouse had been cream colored with little flowers on it when she'd left the house this morning. Now it was stained a rust color. There wasn't an inch on it that wasn't bloodied. The bullet hole was just over where her heart might have been. Pulling the still wet shirt to her chest, she looked at Julia.

"She's my little girl. My baby girl." Julia took her into her arms and held her while Mercedes sobbed. "That monster shot her. Tried to kill his own daughter. And now he tells me that your son has claims on her. She's just a baby, Julia. A little girl."

"Oh honey, I know that. But you got it all wrong. It doesn't work that way when children meet their mates. They grow up. They have time." Mercedes sat down, and Julia sat beside her as she continued. "Patrick told us this morning that he'd found her, his mate. I never dreamed...well, it matters little what I thought at the time. I was happy for him, but afraid too. Like you are. It's not usual for us to find human counterparts, you see."

"She's too young to have a mate and all that goes with it. I know...Darin has shown me what mates can be to each other. I don't want her hurt, not by this." Julia took her hand in hers and put it on Bonnie's chest. Even from where he was, Darin could see her hand moved up and down with Bonnie's breaths. "She's really going to be all right?"

"Oh yes. More than all right. She'll be stronger than she was before. Not ever get sick or any kind of human disease. And since my husband helped convert her, she'll be stronger still. His biting her gave her more than any other wolf could have given her. To be honest, it's more than likely the only reason that she made it." Mercedes asked Julia about the bite. "Never you mind about that now. Just be glad that they were with her. Had they not been there, even having a doctor right there would not have saved her."

Mercedes took Bonnie's hand in hers and watched her daughter. Darin looked at Patrick when he said his name. The boy was going to have to come to realize that he was going to touch Bonnie and he was going to have to get used to it. The three of them, Paddy too, stepped into the hallway to talk quietly.

"The man that hurt her, he's dead. I...my wolf, he killed him before I thought about what I was doing. I'm not even sure I could have stopped myself or even wanted to stop." Darin took his hand and shook it. "She begged me not to let her die, Mr. Douglas. I think she knew she was. She kept telling me to tell you two that she loved you. I couldn't let her go. Not without trying to save her. You should have seen her. She was as pale as the moon and as cold as death."

He held the young man while he cried. Darin wanted to sob too. He owed this kid everything for his quick thinking and actions. There was no doubt that he'd saved her for them, for all of them.

"We love her as well. And her mom is right. She's our little girl. But she's going to be living with us, Patrick. In my home, where my brothers and I are going to hold her. Her grandda too. There are a lot of people that are going to hug her simply because of what we are, and we love her. Are we going to have a problem with that?" Patrick looked at Bonnie in the other room, then at him again. "You're going to have to tell me now, Patrick. I won't have you jumping me every time I try to hug my daughter."

"My wolf is calm with that. He knows that you're stronger than us. He also knows that she's a child, your child. All he wants to do is make sure that she's well and safe." Darin told him he'd make sure of that as well. "I know you will. I know that. I don't know about later, when she's mine. That's a long way off. So maybe by then he'll be okay with it too."

Darin had no idea and said that to him. He'd never known anyone that had found their mate at such a young age. His parents had, but he'd been so young when they'd died that he'd never got to talk to them about it. He wasn't even sure what he might have said.

Mercedes sat with Bonnie the rest of the day. No one mentioned Patrick and his claim on her, and Darin spoke off and on throughout the day to first Paddy, then Julia. Julia had the most information for him, some of it scary. When the rest of his family showed up, they were made as welcome as he'd been.

"What happens to her now?" Jace had asked him, but he just looked at Julia. He didn't have any idea but was glad that someone had brought it up.

Aunt Georgie and the other women had gone to sit with Bonnie and Mercedes, but he and his brothers, along with Miles—Bonnie's grandda—were out on the front porch talking to Julia. Darin wanted to go be with her as well, but he was sure when Bonnie was better, there were going to be things asked and he wanted to make sure he had at least a few of the answers.

"She'll grow up. Mature like before she'd been converted. There will be a few differences. She'll be healthier than humans will be. No childhood disease, as I said to Mercedes. She'll be stronger too." Darin asked Julia about her wolf. "She'll be able to shift, like one of us. I'm not sure if she'll have to wait until she's older, but I don't think she will. I'd like for her to wait awhile before she tries. She lost a great deal of blood, and I think she'll be a tad on the weaker side. Being that she was changed by an alpha of the pack, she'll also have powers that others in the pack won't."

Mason asked about her relationship to Patrick. "He claimed her when he changed her. No other wolf male will touch her. If they do, then they know that it will be certain death. And she'll have us, the entire pack, at her call. Julia and I will treat her as our own when she's here, and she'll be able to call to us, much like you can your aunt when you need her." Paddy handed him a book. The wolf on the cover gave him an idea what the book was going to be about. "You give that to her when she's ready. And you and Mercedes should read it as well. It will give you a better understanding of what she's going to face. Nothing so traumatic as her conversation was, but there will be challenges."

"And the relationship between her and Patrick? What happens with that? I'm assuming that he'll wait until she's old enough to know better." Paddy nodded and smiled at him. "Mercedes is terrified, and if you want to know the truth, so am I. Not that he'll hurt her, but that...well, they're both just kids."

"They are. And I've only known of one other childhood mating, and that was long ago. They grew up together, my parents did. My dad never left her side, and she and him were the greatest of friends long before they came together as man and wife." Paddy handed him two framed pictures. "That one was when they were younger. I guess my dad was about eight, my mom a few years older at twelve. Patrick is only a couple of years older than Bonnie at twelve himself. The other picture is of them after they were wed. My mother was just shy of her twenty-fourth birthday, my dad twenty. Even knowing that they were mates, they never acted on anything sexual until they were both ready. Mom always said it was like she knew that he was hers and that he would be for the rest of her days, and they saw no reason to rush things. I think they had the most dedicated and loving marriage of anyone I ever knew or have known since. I have a feeling that those two will have the same kind of love for each other. And she's a wolf now, so her wolf will take care that she's all right too."

When they were called to supper, neither Mercedes nor Patrick left Bonnie. Darin made a tray for them both and took it to them. After a bit of encouragement, they both ate a little, and he was glad to see that someone had given Mercedes the book. She was reading it when he came to take the trays away sometime later.

At midnight Patrick left to go on a run with his dad then shower after. Darin sat where he'd been sitting. Darin wished he could do more for them both, but knew at this point, it was out of his hands. Mercedes spoke in a low voice as she held onto Bonnie's hand.

"Nash is going to pay for this. I want to go and find him now, but I know that he'd only kill me." Darin said nothing but watched her carefully. She was so upset, and he was worried for her. "He actually tried to have his own daughter killed."

"Patrick said that he was going to take her, this man Rocky. He said that it wasn't until he attacked him to get Bonnie away from him that she was shot. Patrick thinks that his plan was to take Bonnie and then try to get you to come to him." Mercedes asked him how he might have known that. "When he bit the man to...to get him away from Bonnie, he could see his thoughts. Yes, your ex did send him there to get Bonnie, but he was only to take her, not kill her. Nash was going to kill her in front of you to bring you to heel."

"What happens now, Darin? Do the police arrest him for this? Does he go back to prison so that he can manipulate my life from long distance? He has before. Nash won't stop until he gets what he wants."

Darin had spoken to Mason, and they all agreed that Nash was a walking dead man. He just might not know it as yet. "The police can't be called." She asked him why not. "Because Rocky was killed by a wolf. And if even one person gets wind of that, every human that owns a gun will be hunting for them. Not just the wild ones either, but all of them. We deal with Nash our way."

"And what does that mean? You hunt him down? Tear him apart so that.... I want him to pay for this, Darin. Our little girl could have died." He had nearly missed the rest of what she'd said, his mind focusing on the word "our." "I will hunt him down myself if you think I'm going to just let this go."

"We won't. I swear to you that we won't." She stared at him. "Zach is looking for where he might be staying. We know that he's close. The car that Rocky was in had local plates on it. Once we find him, then we'll bring him out in the open and take care of him, pack style. He'll never leave the area alive. This I can promise you."

"You're going to kill him." Darin nodded and told her he was. "Why can't you do it now? Why are you waiting to bring him here?"

"He's a human with humans around him. A pack of wolves and cougars that attack him will be noticed. As much as I don't care about the man, I do about my family. Also, you should know that Emma is looking into a few things, as well as Holly. Susie too. She is...well, you don't want to know what she's doing right now."

"I do want to know." Darin told her what he knew. "You mean she's picking over his dead body and looking into his past? How is that...? This is sort of what she does with the horses, isn't it? She can read their minds and thoughts. But he's dead. His mind is sort of...well, I would think it's sort of lost to her."

"I don't know really how she does it. And, honey, there are no body parts left of Rocky. Not much anyway. The pack took care that no one would ever find anything about him here." He watched her face and knew when she got it. "Right. They have destroyed all traces of his death, and not one of them will say a word about it. Bonnie is in their pack now, and they protect what they consider their own."

"You keep telling me that. All I can see is that they failed her when she needed them most." He didn't comment. She was distraught, and he knew that she was lashing out. When she spoke again, he could tell that she was sorry, but he also knew this was hard on her. "I wasn't fair. This was no one's fault but Nash's, and I didn't mean to say that. Patrick saved her life."

"He did." As they sat there, he told her what he'd found out about what had happened. Most of it she'd been told already, but he knew that she'd not heard much of it. As he got to the part where they'd changed her, she got up and went to the window and looked out.

"Mr. Rose was out at the ranch today. He was looking over the two foals that had been born while he'd been here."

Darin said that he'd talked to him as well and decided that if she wanted to change the subject, he would help her. "Susie said that he put in an order for a dozen more horses. One of them is the foal, I guess." She nodded. "Jessie told me I should have seen Mr. Rose's face when he got back from the ranch. He'd never seen a man so happy before. And I swear I think he did a little dance as he was telling me on the phone about you bringing him into the world."

"The man must be made of money. He tried to tip me for being there to help the ranches. He handed me a thousand dollars like it was nothing to him." Darin didn't point out that it more than likely wasn't all that much to him. "Mason gave me my first check today. It's more than I made in a year as a vet at the clinic."

"They want to make sure you stay here. You want to, don't you?" She looked at him, and he had to laugh at the expression on her face. "I'm just making sure."

"I don't want to leave here. I love this place and all the people in it." He asked her to come to sit with him. "Just let me finish this, okay? I want to stay here. I do, but I'd like some...there are a few things that I'd like to have first. Not in any sort of order, but just a few things. First of all, I want you to change me into a cat. I know that's a big order, but that's what I want."

"All right. I was going to talk to you about it anyway. You should talk to Emma about it, and Holly. Susie was born a cat so she can tell you some things about the conversion, but not like the others can." She nodded. "What else?"

"I want children. With you. And I'll have to talk to her about it, but I want you to adopt Bonnie. If you want to. I know that she's another man's child, but I don't want her to think that, even for a minute, when we have children of our own." Darin didn't get the chance to say anything before she continued. "Also, I know that everyone has been calling me Douglas, and as much as I love that name, I want you to make it legal if you don't mind. Holly said that her and Mason were married at the court house. That'll be fine by me. But I need...I really need to distance myself from the Crosby name. Also, my dad. I know that he has it in his head that him living with us is sort of temporary, but I'd like to make him as welcome in your home as we can."

Darin stood up. "It's your home too. And Bonnie's. And if you want the entire neighborhood to come and live with us, then I'm happy if you are. I'm not so sure about Fox, but I have a feeling that he'd be content as well with the extra people to cook for." He moved toward her, watching her as he thought of all the things she wanted. "I'd love to adopt Bonnie. I wish I had thought of it before now. But no matter if I do or don't, she is my daughter as much as any that you and I have. I shall never treat her any differently than children of my body, and none of my family will either. She's family. Children. I was thinking a dozen or so more if you're up to the challenge."

"Dozen? No, I don't think so." She grinned at him when he pulled her into his arms. "I was thinking at least half that many more. But I want them as a cougar. I want to give them as much of a head start in life as we can give them, and them being cats will help them. Oh Darin, I'm so glad that you came into our lives."

"I am as well, love. Every day I have with you is like a slice of heaven here on earth. I love you so very much." He held her, even after he sat down. Darin watched Bonnie rest and knew that they'd all be better now. Because Nash was going to die.

CHAPTER 10

"Rocky Bends? I'm sorry, I've never heard of that name before. You say that he gave you this address as his own?" Nash held onto the door tightly. The urge to pull his gun and shoot the officer in front of him was overwhelming. But he knew that someone somewhere knew that he was here, and it would only be a matter of time before he was converged upon. "I'm sorry I can't help you with that. Poor guy must be off his head a little, huh?"

Nash wanted to ask about Rocky. It had been three days since he'd called him to tell him that he was bringing the brat to him. He even sent him a picture of her, just to show him the prize was he was getting. Then nothing.

No phone calls, no visits. Up until this police officer had shown up, he'd thought the man had taken the kid off somewhere and was doing his best to her. Nash had been angry when he'd opened the door to the house, thinking it was going to be Rocky telling him how he'd fucked up and already killed her. The man had a need for killing like everyone else did for breathing.

"We're just checking out as much information as we can right now." Nothing. No information and nothing to go on. "You hear from this man, you'll let us know."

"Sure. I'll do that." As he started to close the door, the man turned back to him. It scared Nash a little how the man seemed to be looking for some clue on his body. And when he inhaled deeply, Nash had the frightening urge to run. Like the man was smelling him for some reason, and that Nash was going to be hurt by it. "You need anything else?"

"Nope. I think I've got it all. You have a nice day, Mr. Crosby." It wasn't until the man was gone and the door locked behind him that Nash realized what he'd called him. Not Donaldson, like was on the mail box out front, but his real name.

"Mother fuck." Nash started for the bedroom to pack. He was going to have to go and regroup and find another way to get to Mer. But as soon as he was across the hallway and about five feet from the stairs, he saw the big cougar. Stilling, not even lowering his foot to the floor, he watched him. Nash knew that if he reached for his gun, he was as good as dead. The man walking up behind the cat made his balls feel like they moved up around his throat.

"Hello, Nash. I've come to talk to you. Not that I think it will do any good. So I'm not going to stand here and tell you what I want you to do. Both of us know that you're going to go ahead and force my hand so that I end up killing you." Nash asked him if he was going to sic the cat on him. "No. When you're killed, and you will be, it will be by my hand and not my brother's."

"Brother?" Nash pointed to the cat and froze again when he growled at him. "You say that you're related to a cougar? How the fuck does that even come into play?"

"Does it matter?" Nash supposed that it really didn't. "My name is Darin Douglas, by the way. This is Mason. He's here...well, he didn't want me to come alone, and this way if you get stupider, he can take care of you. I'd like to do it, but I'm thinking he'll be faster and I'd be shit out of luck."

"So you and your brother the cat are here for what reason? I'm assuming you think you can get something from me. I can tell you right now that I'm not going to give you shit. No matter how many animals you bring here." Darin looked to his right, and Nash nearly whimpered. There just in the doorway to the dining room was a giant fucking brown bear. He was laying on the floor like he was ready for a nap, but he looked like he was anything but relaxed. Then Darin said his name and pointed to the other doorway, the one that went to the library. He watched as a wolf, this one bigger than any dog he'd ever seen, sat down. "The bear is my assistant, Jessie Edwards. The wolf is Paddy Sexton, the local alpha. And like I said, this is Mason, my brother."

Tricks with mirrors. Nash wasn't sure how he was doing it, but that had to be it. Mirrors. When he took a step toward the wolf, the thing stood up, his hair standing on end, and swiped at him. The cut in his leg had Nash revising his opinion of how they were in the house and plastering himself against the door behind him.

"What the fuck are you doing with wild animals in my house? Are you fucking insane? They'll hurt someone." Darin laughed, and Nash started to reach for his gun. Almost as soon as he thought about it, there was a breath of air around him and a man standing by Darin with Nash's gun in his hands.

"This would be my friend Monroe. He's a vampire. And you might want to ask yourself how much you've pissed him off by requiring that he come out during the day to disarm you."

Nash watched them. He wasn't sure what scared him more: the fact that this Darin had control over some pretty scary animals or that he was telling him that a vampire was in his — Something occurred to him, and it made Nash smile.

"He's not a fucking vampire. I know because he can't be here. I didn't fucking invite him in. I know my lore. I have to ask him to come in before he can be inside." Nash was pretty proud of himself. And if he was right, then all of this was bullshit.

The man was suddenly standing in front of him, his hand around his throat. And when he lifted him one-handed off the floor, Nash felt his bladder let go.

"This is not your home, and the owner is dead. I may come and go as I please. And you will find out that I do pretty much as I please all the time."

It wasn't that the man was holding him a good foot off the floor that had him terrified. No, it was the teeth, the long fangs that seemed to look sharper the longer he held him there.

When he was back on his feet, Monroe stared at him, then stepped back. Nash had a horrific feeling that the man knew everything there was to know about him. When he looked down at the piss-stained carpet, Nash felt like running to a corner and hiding in it. He wanted to suck his thumb too. Sit in a corner and suck his thumb like he'd done as a child. Darin laughed when the vampire backed away from him.

"I've come to tell you — well, warn you — away from my wife. I know that you're not going to do as you're told, but I've come here in hopes that I won't have to kill you. And make no doubt, I will kill you should you touch her or my daughter." Nash started to ask him what the fuck he was talking about when the man snapped his fingers like he'd forgotten something. "Oh. My wife is Mercedes Douglas. You remember her. She divorced you some years ago. My daughter is Bonnie Crosby, soon to be Douglas too. You're to stay away from them."

"Mer? You think Mer is your wife?" Nash laughed when the man nodded. "You came all the way here to warn me off my own wife, and now you try and tell me that you're married to her? You're out of your mind. Mer is mine until I say differently. And I haven't. Nor will I let her go to marry anyone else. She's going to be my wife until death do her part."

"Why do you think that you still have this hold over her? Or for that matter, why I should give a shit that you think you do? I really would like for you to tell me why you've jumped your parole and come all the way here to get your ass handed to you. She no longer belongs to you. She is not your wife. And you will not harm her again." There was a tone there, one that said you're just too stupid to understand so let me say it slowly for you. But Nash only laughed at the man. "I have warned you, I want you to remember that."

"Yes you have. And fat lot of good it's going to do you. And that brat, Bonnie? You can't have her either. She's my kid." He'd forgotten that she had that stupid name. It was why he'd called her brat all the time. "You get your little farm animals all gathered up and get out of here. I have a man on that right now."

Darin nodded to Monroe, and he moved so quickly that it nearly made him sick to his stomach. But when a Baggie was handed to him, Nash took it without thinking. He asked what was in the bag as he started to open it.

"Your man, Rocky, if that's who you had on it. Or what's left of him that we could find." The bloodied pieces of meat made his belly jump again. He could see bits of hair, a wallet that was torn to shreds. There was a finger, too, with a ring on it…the one that he knew Rocky wore on his pinky finger of his left hand. "I had to look for ten minutes for that much of him. The wolf pack was terribly upset when Rocky there tried to kill one of their mates. But I did think you'd need proof that he was dead."

Nash looked at the wolf, and he yawned. It was not like a person would have done, but he'd shown all of his teeth. They were sharp and dark, like they were stained with things that Nash didn't want to think about. And when he'd stretched, his long claws biting into the wood floor, it was all Nash could do not to piss himself again.

He had to get them out of here. Nash needed to regroup, to plan. He wasn't worried that they'd keep him from his wife, but they were here now, with animals, and he needed to think. Nash wasn't going to walk away from this, not for any reason. Not when he was so close to getting what he wanted.

"You expect me to believe that this is Rocky? You think that I'm just gonna say to you, oh yeah, how right of you. I'll take the next train out. Fuck you." He tossed the bag at the man and wasn't surprised when everything fell out and stained the floor along with his own piss. "You think you can just come in here, tell me a farfetched story, and I'm going to run with my ass covered? You don't know me very well if you think that. Get out of my house. And take this zoo with you. And you can tell that wife of mine that I'm going to expect her to be back home by tomorrow. This shit is going to get her hurt."

The man was gone. Just simply gone, and in his place was a cougar. Not as big as the one that had lain at his feet, but scarier. In his effort to get away from the big cat, Nash fell on the floor in his own piss. Turning over to fend for himself, he felt the big claws bite deeply into his chest, as if the man was going to tear his heart out with his bare claws. Monroe knelt down on his knees and laughed.

"You have really pissed this one off, in the event that you didn't realize that." Nash told him to get him off him. "I don't think so. I think my friend Darin here has a few words to say to you. I would have simply killed you, but then he's a man who thinks there are good humans in the world, while I do not. I would like to think he's going to get through to you, but I know that you're stupid."

"Get the fuck off of me." Nash put his hands on the cat's face to force him off and was bitten. The cat didn't let him go either, but held his hand in his mouth like he was going to take it off. "Tell him to get out of here now and I won't hunt him down and kill him."

"If you honestly think that he's going to do that, then you are much stupider than we all thought. Anyway, he'll smell you coming now. And I'll be around to warn him should you sneak by the others. Now, listen up, he's speaking to me." When Monroe paused, Nash thought of all the ways that he was going to hurt these men. "He said to tell you that now that he has a connection to you, a blood one, he can read your mind. Darin wanted me to tell you that if you think you're going to even get to do half that shit in your head, then you aren't listening to him. Or me for that matter."

"I'm going to kill you all." Monroe nodded and looked at the cat again. "What is he saying now? No doubt something profound that is going to leave me quaking in my boots."

Nash was free. The cat was off him. The vampire or whatever he was had moved as well. Nash sat up and looked around the room, and realized that not only had the other cougar left, but the bear had as well. The wolf and the cat were the only animals left besides the vampire.

"Darin said to tell you that if you don't back off and leave town, not only will he enjoy killing you, but he'll make sure you suffer as much as you made his wife." Nash snorted. This shit was getting old. "Do you have a death wish? Do you have any idea what a shifter does when someone harms their family? If I were you, I'd run until—"

"Yeah, well, you're not me and I don't scare easily." Monroe only looked down at his stained pants, and Nash stood up. "I have some kidney issues. So what? I had an accident. It'll be the last time you see me like this."

"No doubt. But for some reason I don't think we have the same ideas about how that will come into play." The cat stood up and moved to the door and out of his house, the wolf right behind him. Nash asked Monroe if they were done. "For now. I would like to tell you that I hope you have your affairs in order. Also to tell you a few things that you may or may not be aware of just yet. The houses that you owned are no longer yours to call home. Poor Rocky won't be getting them either. I don't believe he has any use for them now. Oh, and the offshore money too. I do hope that you didn't have any plans for that money. It's going for a very good cause. Bonnie will need a bit of money to go to college someday if she wants. That, and all your other accounts have been emptied. I so enjoyed that more than you can know. Mercedes will put it all to good use, I'm sure."

Nash said nothing. He was too busy trying to figure out how they'd known about his accounts. And when the man disappeared, just seemed to vanish without so much as a puff of air, Nash stood up and locked the doors.

Going to his office when he finished that, he pulled out his laptop and opened up his accounts. It only took him twenty minutes to realize that not only had they gotten to his offshore account like Monroe had said, but his bank accounts were empty too. All four of them. Nash was broke as of right fucking now.

~~~

Miles watched his granddaughter while she sat at the desk and did her homework. He'd been trying all day to talk to her, ask her about her new self, but he wasn't sure how to do it. Miles had missed a lot of years with his only granddaughter, and now he wasn't sure how to talk to her. When Fox came in the room with them and handed him a plate of cookies and a cup of tea, he asked Bonnie to join them at the small table. Miles was so nervous when she joined him that he was sure she could hear his heart pounding.

"Are you afraid of me?" He looked at Fox, who winked and left them. Miles looked at Bonnie and tried to think how to tell her that he was. "I won't hurt you. I won't hurt any of you."

"I'm afraid this is a little more than one old man can handle all in one day." She nodded and put her hands under the table like she was afraid of upsetting him more. "I'm not so much afraid of you as I don't understand this. I mean, I've known about shifters, but I've never had much to do with them before moving here with you guys."

"You've been seeing them every day since you were brought here, Grandda. Darin and his brothers are all shifters. And that man Monroe that came here earlier, he's a vampire. You've been around them a long time. So what is it about me that scares you?" He wasn't sure where to begin. He wanted to tell her that he was more afraid for her than of her. Miles wanted to tell her that he didn't know her well and now she was something different, something that while he knew of, he didn't understand. "Don't be afraid of me."

"I'm not, not really. Scared, but not of you." He decided that was right. "You and I, we've not had a lot of time to get to know each other. Your momma, she hid me away to keep that monster from.... I'm sorry. I know that he's your father and all, but—"

"No, he's not my father. Just the man who helped make me. But I think Mom thought she was doing the right thing, don't you?" He said that she'd saved his life. "And Patrick saved mine by doing this to me. Had he not, then I'd not be here at all. And I want you to know that I really want to be here. I don't want you afraid that I'll hurt you, though."

Miles tried to think how to say what had been inside his heart and mind since she'd come down the stairs this morning. He loved her...loved his daughter and his granddaughter so much. And he'd been trying to get to know her, but things had been getting in his way. The chair he was attached to was the biggest problem.

"When she hid me away, I was so mad at her. I wanted to call her right up and tell her that I could fend for myself, that I wanted to protect her. Even when she sat down with me and told me all the things that man had done to her, I was still angry. I knew that I could help her, that with her being young and healthy, she'd not been able to keep him from hurting her, but I was a grown man. But she told me that if anything happened to me, she'd just die. I believed her." Bonnie took his hand in hers and he felt her love. He kissed it before continuing with his story. "Then one day I fell out of my chair. I lay there thinking that had she been there, if my daughter had been with me, then I'd not have to be lying on the floor, I'd be helped up by her. Then it hit me. Christ almighty, I couldn't get up. How was I gonna help her?"

"He would have killed you. Like he tried to kill me." He nodded and held her hand to his cheek again. "When I was dying, I thought of you. I mean, not much, I'm sorry to say, but I did. I thought how sad it was that I'd not gotten to know you. That we'd not gone to get ice cream together, and that I'd miss when you made me little notes in my lunch."

"You never said anything about them. I thought that you'd thought me an old fool." Bonnie shook her head, and he felt tears fill his eyes. "Your grandmother would have been so proud of you. And this thing with you being a wolf, you know what she would have said? She'd have said, Miles Fisher, what is wrong with you being like this? You have her still, don't you? And then she'd go on about me not having enough years left to be an old fool."

"I'm afraid too, if you want to know the truth. I have this mate that I don't know all that well that I'm going to spend the rest of my life with. I have a big pack at my beck and call too. And I can change into a wolf with only a thought." He asked her not to do that just yet. "No, I won't. Paddy said I had to be stronger yet. I'm still tired a lot from all the blood loss."

"I love you, darling. More than I ever thought a man could love a little girl." Bonnie told him that she loved him as well and would always.

Miles talked to her for the rest of the afternoon. Darin called once to say that he was running behind and might be late to dinner, and then Mercedes called to tell them that she was helping a birthing. It looked like it was just going to be the two of them for a little while longer.

Making their way into the kitchen, Miles told Fox what was going on. He was kneading bread at the big counter and said that if they wanted a snack before dinner, he'd make them something. Miles said he'd get it and rolled around the kitchen getting supplies from the fridge that had been set on the lower shelf just for him. He and Bonnie had crackers and cheese while they sat in the kitchen talking to Fox.

Mason entered the back door about twenty minutes later and tipped his big black hat at them all before snagging a few crackers and cheese for himself. As he stood there talking to Fox about something on the ranch, Miles thought of something that he'd not realized until that very moment. He lived on a ranch.

"I'd like to ride a horse." He'd blurted it out so quickly that he'd been embarrassed to have interrupted the two men talking. "I'm sorry. I was just thinking about horses and cattle, and I realized that I've never been on one. I've never even been near one."

"I rode over here on one. Come on out and I'll help you out." Before he could protest too much, he was in the yard in his chair and sitting by the biggest creature he'd ever seen. Christ, he must have been insane to think he wanted to get on one of these. "Now, I'm gonna lift you up on the saddle and you hang on. Bonnie here is going to get up behind you and help you hang on if you can't manage it on your own."

"Oh, she might get hurt." Mason assured him that she could take a fall better than he could. "Oh yes, her being a wolf. I forgot."

Being lifted by the man who he'd come to admire was amazing. Miles knew that he didn't weight nearly as much as he had when he'd been healthy, but Mason had picked him up and set him in the saddle like he'd weighed nothing more than a baby did. As soon as he felt the power of the animal under him, Miles was beginning to have third and fourth regrets.

"He won't move until I tell him to. You just get used to having your body up there and we'll take it slowly." Miles nodded and held onto the saddle where he'd been told and gripped it tight enough to have his fingers cramp up. "Now, your feet are in the stirrups. I'm to understand that you have no power in your legs, but you can feel some things, right?"

"I can feel the horse, but I can't move my legs, correct." Mason told him what he was going to do. "Okay, but don't go fast. I'm not thinking that I'm a great horseman like you are."

"You just hold on, Miles. The horse won't throw you." Miles nodded, holding onto the saddle for all he was worth. "You won't fall. You're as safe as I am up there. Old Brindle here, he likes to run, but he's a might worn out by carrying my big butt around the ranch all day."

Miles nodded again as he was led around the yard. He supposed he should have felt like a small child at one of those rides at the circus, but he felt...well, whole. The height he was off the ground was dizzying, but it wasn't like he was on a plane. Miles looked around. Christ, he thought, this was why men and women did this.

"You're having fun, huh, Grandpa?" Miles looked at Bonnie, who was walking alongside him and the horse, holding his leg for him. They'd thought she would ride with him, but Mason told him he was doing just fine and dandy. "I loved it the first time I got on one. It felt like I could run forever and never stop."

"I'm not so sure I'm ready for all of that." But he knew what she meant. The wind felt cleaner up here. It wasn't, but it felt like it. The trees were greener, the grass seemed to glow with health. Miles looked at Mason when he handed him the reins and stepped back. "You think I can do this?"

"I don't see why not. You're doing well. And staying put. That's the most important thing, staying on the horse's back." Miles nodded and flicked the long strings of leather gently as he'd been told. "That's it. Just give him his head, and he'll be good to you. You turn him to where you want to go just by a small pull on the side you're planning. But make it a nice fat turn. He's only a horse, as you know."

Miles thought perhaps that this was the greatest gift he could have gotten today. He rode around the yard for twenty minutes, Mason and Bonnie snapping pictures like he was some sort of special rider or the kid he'd thought of earlier at the carnival. He supposed in a way that he was special, though. The ride certainly was for him. When he told Mason that he'd had enough, the man lifted him off the big horse again and sat him in his waiting chair. Bonnie kissed and hugged him and Miles felt tears gather in his eyes.

"You gave an old man a rare treat, Mason. I won't forget this." Mason nodded and tipped his hat like he'd seen him do a thousand times since he'd been here. The hat was lowered again, the sun making the big man squint. The hat, like the man, was as much a part of this earth as the trees and the grasses.

Miles could see now that it wasn't a decoration to this man, nor to any of the Double Deuce workers. It was a part of their uniform of boots with holes in them, jeans in just as bad shape. He noticed that gloves were always in good repair, and hats were forever near them to put on when they were out of doors.

He was as sure as he was sitting there that Mason's hat had a long story. It was worn in places, the leather of it lighter in places where Mason would touch it to be adjusted for his needs. The string around it had long since been replaced with a brown tie, but it was no less worn than the black of the hat. There were no decorations on it, no silver stars or feathers as he'd seen on other men in the city. This was a hat that was functional. A necessity out here in the harsh country.

These men and women were no less hardened than their forefathers. Just as hardy, and happier for what they did to the earth. Miles thought that if Mason's hat could talk, it would tell a story that would be as heartbreaking as it was funny. Wondrous things would be told to a listener, and Miles was sad that he'd not be able to hear it. Mason shook his hand as he was brought back into the house.

"Well, I'm gonna head on back to the ranch. I have nine calves coming today, and your daughter said I had to be there in the event that we had to help out. She's a mite upset with me today." Miles asked him why. "Well, you'd think it was because I told her to get a better pair of boots to wear in the yards, but I think it's more like I was right and she don't care much for that."

Miles was still laughing when he made his way back in the kitchen area with Bonnie. Life, he decided, was an adventure around here.

CHAPTER 11

Darin wasn't sure he'd ever been this tired before. Rolling to his back, he thought about just trying to sleep for another hour but knew that there were things that needed seen to. There were four guests coming in today, and there was still the matter of hiring a cook. Truman wasn't coming back.

He'd been beaten up pretty badly, and while he was healing he said he wasn't cut out for this sort of work. Darin didn't want to tell him that he thought perhaps he was right, but was glad that he wasn't going to have to tell him that they needed less stress in the kitchen. He'd not noticed how tense it had been there until Julia had started cooking.

Last night he'd gone into the kitchen to snag a sandwich. The dishwashers had some music playing in their area, and were singing along with it. Darin hadn't ever remembered any kind of sounds coming from the kitchen at all, much less singing, when Truman had been there. And just as he was to comment on it, someone dropped a plate. Its breaking sounded all over the room. But instead of screaming at them, which Darin had witnessed Truman do before, Julia made a joke. How she hoped it was one of the dirty ones and not the ones that had been washed up.

The food coming from the kitchen now was homemade. Not to say that Truman didn't cook a good meal, but Julia was putting together dishes such as browned chops with gravy. Pot roast with potatoes and carrots. Just the day before there had been chicken fried steaks, mashed potatoes, and white creamy gravy. Things that he'd enjoyed at home. And the guests had loved every drop of it.

"You're thinking very hard. Did you know that?" He looked over at Mercedes and kissed her on the nose. "Well, that's sort of a disappointment. I was hoping for a nice ride, cowboy."

He lifted her over him and was glad that he'd pulled the sheet off him in a ditched effort to get up. She slid down over his cock when he held it for her and moaned. Darin loved waking up next to this woman more than he'd thought possible. And when he was able to make love to her before his day began, he thought his whole life was better.

"Tell me what you were thinking about." She was naked, on his cock, playing with her breasts. Darin told her that he wasn't capable of thought right now. "I have a thought. Did you know that I can feel every part of you when you're inside of me this way? Your crown is so thick I can feel each curve of it."

"Christ, woman." Darin grabbed her hips and tried to make her ride him faster. "Come on, baby, give me a scream."

"I need this." Her ride slowed, her back bowed with each movement. When she cupped her breasts and pinched her hard nipples again, Darin sat up and took one of them into his mouth and bit her. "That's it, baby, suck me until I come. I need to come all over you so badly."

He cupped her ass, bringing her closer to him with each of her forward motions. He suckled hard on her breasts, teasing one then the other before starting over again. When she wrapped her arms around his shoulders, bringing her body even closer to his, he nuzzled her throat and nipped none too gently on her pounding pulse. Her scream of release had him rolling her to her back and fucking her hard. And when she came again, he bit her, drawing her essence and her blood into his body until he came with her. Darin didn't think he'd ever get enough of her. And didn't even want to try.

He held her to him after rolling to his back again. He was still deep inside of her and rocked up twice before she stretched out her legs alongside of his and looked up at him. Sated for now, he held her to him and thought of nothing in particular. But he did think that if he could just stay here all day long, he might be the happiest man in the world.

"What's the matter?" He kissed her again, and she grinned at him. "You're trying to distract me. What's going on?"

"Let me see. This in no set order, but I have to find a cook today. Jessie wants to have a couple of days off. Jace asked me to come over today and help him with the milker program that was set up in the barns that I have no clue about, but I have a manual that is as thick as a few books I have. Zach bought himself a farm, a real farm that has furrows, not cattle or horses, and wants me there when he asks Mason and Jace if they'll buy his product. Bonnie needs new shoes and clothing. How the hell do you keep a kid in clothes?" She said that it was a trial. "Yeah, speaking of which, I have to go to the court house today to see Emma about something. She said it wasn't bad news, but I don't trust it right now. Your ex-husband is around, and I must say, he is a dick of the highest order. Let me see, did I miss anything?"

"Yes, you love me." He told her that he really did. "And all the other things? Let's make a list of the order in which you can get to them. Oh, and I can do some of it. I'll go to see Jace about the programing. Believe it or not, I know a lot about that. And then Bonnie and I can go to the mall. She's been wanting to have a girls day out and Dad said he wanted to get him a hat. I'm not sure where that came from, but there you go. Julia is the best choice for your kitchen. You know it and everyone else does. Just ask her. I think you might be surprised by the answer she has already in her head."

When she got up and went to the bathroom, Darin just lay there. In less than two minutes she'd cut his list of shit going on in half. He reached out to his brother Jace and told him what had just happened.

Yeah, Holly does that all the time. I won't even have to tell her what I have on my plate and she'll come in and say she's done this or that for me and I just mark it off. Having a mate is a hell of a lot better than I ever thought it would be, and not just for the mind blowing sex either. Darin agreed with him. *About today and the milkers...are you coming, or is your lovely wife?*

She said she has come by knowledge about them, so I guess she's coming. Christ, I have so much to do. I have to go and talk to Julia first. He told him about Truman and his thoughts as he made his way to the other shower in their room. *I never realized what a hard ass he'd been.*

Rules. Some people just can't seem to bend them a little. He always struck me as a rigid sort of guy. A nice one, but stiff all the same. Darin was beginning to see that too. *Julia will more than likely take the job if you ask her. Paddy was saying how much fun she was having at it, and that she was a hell of a lot more relaxed at home too. I think that alone will sell her on taking it. Not to mention the money coming in. I told you about that, right? That the pack was having a little trouble?*

Yes, but I thought it eased a bit since the other businesses were in town. Jace said it helped, but their household was suffering. *I'm going to call her as soon as I get to work. Thanks.*

After getting out of the shower and dressed, he went to the kitchen to find Miles and Bonnie already there. He asked where Mercedes was.

"She had to make a few phone calls. And Aunt Emma called. She wanted to know if you could bring in Mom when you come to see her. She said that it had to do with some money. I told Mom and that's why she making some calls." Darin nodded and sat down to eat. Fox had made him a huge breakfast, and he was going to try and eat every bit of it. There was no telling when he'd get to eat again. "Oh, and I was wondering if I could have you take me to the mall without Mom. Saturday is her birthday."

Darin looked at Bonnie while she dug into her own breakfast of cereal. She'd said it so calmly that he wondered if she was giving him a hint or that she thought he already knew. Looking at Miles, he had a feeling that he understood that he'd not a clue when his own mate's birthday had been.

"She loves flowers to plant in the ground. And pretty frames. I don't think I've seen her taking pictures lately, but she used to do that all the time." Darin nodded, making a mental list to make it to the jewelry store as well as the mall with Bonnie. "Don't get her anything practical. She might tell you that's what she wants, but she hasn't had anyone buy her things but myself and Bonnie, and she might need a little pampering. After all this, I think she could use that more than she might a new sweeper. Though I don't think she'd get to use it, not with Fox around."

"No sweeper. Yeah, I can do that." No you can't, his mind screamed at him. To Bonnie he said he'd pick her up after school and they'd go then. Darin did the only thing a desperate man could do and reached out to his new sisters for help. He called Holly on his way into work after having to promise his truck all sorts of strange things to get it to start for him.

"Well, her daddy said pampering, right? You should buy her a day at the spa. For all of us." Holly said that it would be a girl's day out. "And Bonnie and Georgie too. The six of us could have such a wonderful time, and we'd make sure that she has a blast. Then you can take her out to a really nice place to eat, and maybe a concert or something. Oh, wait, the opera. I think she mentioned that she's never been to one."

He asked her how to get tickets to that, and she said she'd take care of it for him. The rest was up to him. As he made his way to work he made some calls, and not only did he get the day booked for the six of them, Holly had managed to get two box seats from Emma that he could use, a limo to pick them up and take them around town, and even a fitting for a dress for Mercedes to wear. Darin was going to be in the poor house, but he was excited to have been able to do this for her. He just hoped that the rest of his day was this easy.

~~~

Jace watched as Mercedes programmed the computer. The cows were getting impatient, and he really didn't blame them. This was the third time that she'd shown him how to do this, and he was getting impatient as well. Jace thought that he liked the old way much better, where he hooked the cows up to the cups and went about his day for about an hour. Then returned to do it all again.

"See this?" He looked at the computer screen. He watched as the little light beeped. "That is cow number fourteen. She's right there in stall ten. See?"

"Yes. And not to be an ass, but so?" She laughed and he did as well. "I think this was a mistake on my part. I have no idea what the hell I'm doing."

"Yes you do. Look. As soon as she puts her head in the stall, the computer will take over." Number fourteen moved to the harness as she'd been doing most of her life, and her head was clamped in place. Not tightly, but enough that she'd not back away when things were started. The cups came out of the floor under her and were attached to her teats, and he heard the computer make a noise and watched as the amount of milk was registered on the screen. "You'll know right to the ounce how much milk she gives you and what the grade is. I'm not sure what that is, but I'm sure you do."

He answered her question without thinking. "Grade is the cream of the milk. So when this is done, the milk will go to the storage bins like it did before?" She nodded, and they watched as three more cows were brought in and set up. The machine could handle as many as two dozen cows at a time, but they were taking it slow today. "And once it's there, it divides it up by grade of milk?"

"Yes. The dairy, I understand, is ready to open up for business today too. You're going to make your first batch to use." He nodded and rubbed the tightness in his belly. "You do know that this is going to be huge, don't you? With the new businesses in town, there will be more people coming in to buy products to take home. Especially things that are made right here in town. And Logan said you have it set up for tours at some point."

"Yes. Later though. Right now we're just getting our feet wet. The guys that have come in to help us get it right, they said that Douglas/McBride cheese will be in every household in the state soon. Christ, this was a terrible idea." He rubbed his belly harder. She took his hand away from it and told him to look at the screen.

Fourteen was gone. All the stalls were full now, and the milking was moving right along. Not only had it been a great deal faster, but cleaner as well. He moved to stand behind one of the workers and asked him how the cows were doing.

"Great. Margaret is moving around like she's the queen of the barn. And the rest of them are lined up ready to take their turns. They sure are liking how fast they can get in and out to the hay again." Jace asked him who Margaret was. "Oh, number fourteen. And my mother-in-law. Fourteen reminds me of her. As big as she is, too."

Jace was still laughing as the next set of cows were brought in to be milked. At this rate, they'd be done in less time than it would have taken him to do half the herd. He was liking this better and better all the time.

"Darin said that you were going to install these at the other barn too. That you'd be able to not just increase your production, but that you'd be able to have more cows than you had before this." Jace told her that they were going to take it slow, but that was the plan. "And the other farmers? Are they gonna get on the band wagon and try this method out as well? I don't see that happening, just so you know."

"Why not?" He looked at the production and called the dairy to ask for a truck to be sent. They had their first truck load ready to make into cheese. When he realized that Mercedes hadn't answered, he looked at her. "Why don't you think anyone will want to do this?"

"Money. I mean, I know that you married into money, so did Mason, but the rest of the town, they don't have that much to put into this sort of equipment. Which I think is a good thing." He asked her why again. "Well, at the rate you're growing, all of you, by this time next year you'll be able to help the town grow more by hiring most of the townspeople to work for you. You're diversified enough that there will always be something to talk about at the dinner table too."

"You mean if, say, a husband and wife work for us, one might be a dairy farmer with us while someone else might help out with the beef end of the family businesses." She asked about Zach. "What about him? He works for both ranches. I'm sure he can find something else to talk about."

"He has a farm now." Jace leaned against the pole and waited. "I think he's going to grow grain and hay. To sell. I guess he got a great deal on the place and was hoping to make his fortune by selling his wares to the public."

"Do you think he's planning to go public with his grain?" Mercedes said she had no idea, but that it would probably be to whoever wanted to buy it. "Are you, by chance, setting me up for something?"

She looked confused. "What would I be setting you up for? I just heard him talking to Darin the other day, and I thought you knew. Anyway, it's a lovely place. We've been out to the house. It's going to need some work, but I think he's living in the basement for now. He comes by the ranch to take a shower and do his laundry until he can get some of his own things out there. I guess the place has been abandoned for a while, but is in fairly good shape."

"Eleven years or so. The bank owns it, or they did. I never even gave it a thought to.... When did he buy it?" She said a few days ago. "And do you suppose he was going to let us know?"

"To be honest with you, I thought you all knew. But I would imagine he would have told you sooner or later. But I can see why he's put it off." He asked her why. "Well...." Jace waited. He could feel her fear at this. Whether it was because she didn't want to tell him or was afraid of his answer, he decided that he'd not say a word until she did. "Susie told me about what you guys tried to do for her and Gerard. I think he thinks you'd do the same to him. Zach has his heart set on doing this on his own."

"You mean he doesn't want us to take over. You think we'd do that?" She said that she was sure of it. "What would you do? If this were your brother and he'd done something like this?"

"You make it sound as if he's done something wrong. Has he? And so you know, he hasn't. Not as far as I can see. He's a young man, trying his best to live up to his brothers' successes. And if you can't see that, then to hell with all of you. I'm very proud of him. Do you have any idea how hard this has been on him? Doing this and being afraid of your disapproval?" Jace started to deny that when she snapped at him again, this time with a finger poking him in the chest. "You and your brothers have done so well for yourselves. You have a successful ranch, a soon to be successful dairy farm. Horses coming out of the woodwork for you all. And yes, they really do just sort of migrate to the ranch. I've seen them. But to live up to the Douglas fame, it's hard."

"Are you and Darin struggling?" She told him this wasn't about them. "But you are. You're still paying off the debt that Crosby left you, aren't you? And Darin is as well. You two, other than the house, have nothing, do you?"

"The bad credit, it's in my name and it has ruined me. I can't even get a car loan." He knew the exact moment when she realized she'd said too much. "Look, this is about Zach and his new venture. You should be proud of him for what he's taken on. I am."

"I am as well. I just wish that he'd been able to come to me." She didn't say anything but turned back to the computer screen. He'd bet anything that she was thinking of a way to get out of here, but like she said, she didn't have a car. He had thought that they'd purchased her one to use, but would have to talk to Mason about it. He had been sort of out of the loop for a few weeks. "Mercedes, how much in debt are you?"

"Over sixty thousand in credit cards alone. Then there is the car loan that I took out that I never saw the car for, a house that has been foreclosed on, as well as the outstanding bills of my own. The clinic where I worked is suing me now for leaving them without a doctor. I can't seem to get a break." He wanted to hold her. To tell her it would be all right and take care of it for her. But he knew that she'd be pissed off, and that would be worse than seeing her upset like this. "Please don't tell anyone. Darin knows, but no one else does. We're making it, barely, but we have a roof over our heads and hot water. That is more than I thought we'd have at this point in our lives."

After she left, walking back to the clinic on Mason's part of the ranch, Jace stood in his barn and looked around. He'd spent more on this equipment than he had anything in his life. Money had been something that he'd never had growing up. And now that he had it, he still found himself pinching every penny except for when it came to the ranch. But he did have a brand new home, a new truck, and money in his personal accounts if he needed it. Jace decided it was time to have a family meeting. But first he needed to talk to Mason.

After telling him everything he'd found out and some of his speculations on a few others, he and Mason met at his house in the kitchen. It occurred to him then that they did that a lot, met in this part of the house when there was business to discuss. There was a perfectly good office here and at the other houses, but the kitchen was the meeting place. He took the glass of tea and sandwich that were handed to him as he made notes on what they needed to take care of.

"I think that Mercedes is right." Mason nodded as he continued. His brother was stuffing food in his face faster than he was. And Jace thought it was funny. "I can still remember Susie's face when we stepped in and tried to run roughshod over her and Gerard. She put us in our place, and now look. They're making it without our help."

"So what do we do?" Mason didn't say anything. Then he got up and left him. Jace finished his sandwich and was having pie when he returned. Mason handed him a page of handwritten notes that looked like Emma's handwriting. Jace nearly choked when he got to the bottom. "Is this right?"

"Yes. She's more than a hundred grand in debt as of yesterday morning. Darin has made arrangements with a couple of the credit card companies, but for the most part, they just want their money. And I was concerned that they'd take the farm from them, so I had someone look into things. And then Emma and Holly got wind of it and asked for Monroe to help them out with a few passwords." Jace was almost afraid to ask. "That's why they're meeting with her this afternoon."

"Are you going to tell me that Crosby has money? Or he had money?" Mason smiled and nodded. "Christ, I'm almost afraid to ask. Will it be enough to take care of this debt that he put her in?"

"Oh yes, more than enough. And as of this morning, the houses that he had are in Darin and Mercedes's names, as well as a few properties that he hadn't done anything with as yet. His bank accounts are empty. And this account that he had in another country is gone as well. That one is where the bulk of the cash was. Monroe also had a look around the house while he was snooping and found cash stashed all over the place. Millions. He managed to find it all after a little look into the man's head, and found enough for them to live off of for quite some time, just in the house." Jace asked how bad it was going to be for the dickhead. "Essentially, Crosby is dead broke. And the gun that Darin took from him? I turned it over to the police this morning, having just found it on my property. I think it might have a few bits of blood on it, as well as some prints that are going to lead them right to the man." Jace pointed out that the man was on parole. "He is at that. And he's not in his home state, nor is anyone going to be happy that he's been carrying a gun, not to mention that the house he is living in? It's not his either. The body of the man who owned it I'm sure will turn up soon as well."

Jace thought he could get used to helping his family this way. The bad guys got their comeuppance. He wasn't going to be yelled at by his sisters, and money would be Darin's and Mercedes's to spend on things that they wanted and not just what they absolutely needed. As the two of them went out to the barns, he told his brother about the milkers.

Things were looking up for his family, but he hoped that it wouldn't come with a price. He was almost afraid to get his hopes up too far. Lately things had a tendency to go to shit in a heartbeat. But, he told himself, things usually turned out okay, but they did have a long path in getting to that point at times.

CHAPTER 12

Mercedes looked at the check, then at the stack of paperwork in her hand. They were bills, her bills. And they were all marked *paid in full*. She looked at Emma when she realized that she was speaking to her again.

"I'm sorry. But could you just start over? What do you mean, this is from Nash? He wouldn't have given me shit, and we all know that." Darin took the paid bills from her, and she was glad to give them up. There was something really scary about having them in her hands.

"You said that Nash had this much money. In his accounts. How is that even possible? He was stealing from me. He ran up my credit and never paid on them."

"Yes he did. And he did have that much money in his accounts. Enough to pay off the debt that he incurred for you, as well as that extra cash that is in the form of the check you are now holding. And again, there is also an account set up in Bonnie's name so that she can go to the college of her choice. If she decides that she doesn't want to, then she can use it for whatever she wants. I'm sure they could use it to buy a lovely home." Emma smiled at her when she lifted her hand up to stop her. "We found the money in some offshore accounts. Well, Monroe did. He's the one you have to thank for this."

"Are you saying that he stole this money?" Emma asked Darin who he meant, Monroe or Nash. "Nash. He's...Christ, this is a shitload of money. I mean, the paid bills alone are more than we ever hoped to have paid off."

"He's been dealing in drugs and women for a very long time. Even before he met you. Then there is the money that he's paid each month from a few bars and stores that he takes care of. And by that, he lets them do business so long as he gets a huge cut. You'd almost think that he was some sort of drama on television. Mercedes, he has lied to you about a great many things. Most of it about money." Mercedes snorted. No shit that he'd lied to her, she wanted to say to Emma. "The money is just the tip of the iceberg for you guys. There are houses, as well as some property that is in your name now. A few dozen cars that are vintage and could go for a great deal of money as well. If you'd like, I can have my attorney look into selling them off."

When Emma handed her the list of the cars, she handed it to Darin. This was just too much. When she'd been asked to come here, she'd thought that Emma was going to tell her that she had to move out of the big house to live with one of them or in a box. She had one all picked out, a nice sized freezer one that she'd seen in the back of the Douglas House. Not that she wanted that for her daughter or Darin. There was only so much a person would be asked to do, and she and her family living with them would have been too much.

"What does he say about all this? Nash, I mean. I'm betting he's not happy about the turn of events." Emma only smiled at her. "Does he know who did this and where his money went?"

"Oh yes. Monroe made sure that he knew when you were at his house the other day, Darin. He said that he didn't think that he believed him, but he's sure that he does now. And by the way, the house that you visited that day, it belongs to a Mr. Donaldson. His body turned up this morning at a dumpsite just out of town. I think Mason told them that he'd found a gun and there were prints on it. As well as Donaldson's blood. The poor man had been gone for a few days by the time that he was found."

Mercedes started to pace. This was coming together too fast for her and the questions were overwhelming her. Nash had money? Why did he feel the need to charge her accounts then? He'd taken money out of her account too. Why take her little bit of money when he had so much of his own? With the fact that he had houses, more than one it sounded like, why had he let her and his only child live like they had? What sort of cruelty was he working at? When Darin said her name, she looked at him.

"Emma said that he's being arrested in the morning. They're not worried that he'll run. He has no money, and they're pretty sure that he knows his days are numbered anyway. She wants to know if you want to be there when he is." She shook her head. "Bonnie is going to be watched all day tomorrow as well. No one will get to her if he escapes."

"Do you think he will?" No one answered her. "Please tell me that there is going to be some sort of sniper team there when he's taken. I don't think I can handle knowing that one lone cop is going to go and try to bring him in."

"He's going to escape because we want him to. There is no way he'll make it to prison." Mercedes sat down when Emma came from her side of the desk to sit with her on the couch. "If he were to go to prison, do you know what would happen to him? Do you remember what he did to you when he was only in jail for those few weeks?"

"Yes. He had people follow me around. Some of them hurt me, others just did things to me, like knocking food off the shelves when I went to the store. And each of them told me it was from him. That he'd sent them to keep me in line. He was in jail for domestic violence, yet it never stopped with him. He was...they told me that he was living it up. A friend of mine worked in the county court house, and she told me that he had food delivered daily and that he had bottles of expensive wine brought in too. Even a tailor came in to fit him for his suit that he wore on his release day." Emma nodded. "You're hoping that he'll try to get away and someone will shoot him. I don't think that'll work. Nash has a way of landing on his feet all the time."

"He's not going to be shot either. The leap is going to take care of him." Mercedes asked if they were planning to murder him. "Murder a murderer? No, it will be something more along the lines of an attack. I doubt anyone will put much effort into making sure he gets the best of care if he were to survive them. Which I'm not saying he will. He's pissed off a great many people. And that's only from around here."

"You mean to say that their animals are going to tear him apart." Emma just looked at Darin and so did Mercedes. "Please tell me that you're not going to chase this man into an ambush and then kill him. That won't make you any better than he is. You know that, don't you?"

"Mason said that he was going to hang himself by confessing to what he's done. And yes, we'll all be there, but we won't kill him. He'll do that on his own." Mercedes asked him how. "I don't know, love. I'm just telling you what Mason said to me just now. He said that if you want more details, he'd be glad to sit down with us and talk to you about them. I'm actually hoping that you don't. Mason can be pretty...mean when it comes to family."

The mind thingy. She loved it at times, but right now she could gladly tell them all to use conventional ways of talking. Mercedes decided that as soon as she was changed, she was never going to speak to any of them again that way. It was mean to know things that others didn't.

"We're sitting here planning a man's death. Do you know that? Doesn't that bother you in the least?" Darin took her hands into his. "Please don't tell me this is for the best."

"I wasn't. But I'd like to ask you something. Not to be cruel, but just something I'd like to ask. What would you have done to him should he have succeeded in killing Bonnie?" She told him that was cruel. "No, it's not. It's the truth. He sat down with that other man and planned out to the minute how he was going to take our daughter and then kill you and her both. I'm sure that he's still planning that. How he's going to kill you. Make you suffer in ways that you can't imagine. When I spoke to him, he didn't strike me as the type of person who gives up just because the odds are against him. Nor does he like when people tell him no. Is that about right?"

"Yes, he hates to be told anything negative. And has hurt people that have told him that something was not available that he thought he should have." She looked at the bills still in a neat pile on the corner of the desk. "He told me when he forced me to marry him I was going to give him things that he'd ever had. I assumed it was money. Not that I had all that much, but Dad and I were comfortable. But he had it all along, didn't he? What do you suppose he thought that I could give him? It certainly wasn't love. He told me hourly how much he hated me."

"He wanted your submission. And your fear of him. To have you say that you were afraid of him is what he thinks about most." She looked up at Gerard when he came into the room and spoke to her after taking a seat. "I've been with him today, just brushing by him when he thought he wouldn't be recognized. And in doing so, I was able to read his mind. The things that he plans to do to you when he gets you are sickening. And to Bonnie. After he finishes with her, he plans to give her to anyone who wants her. For whatever they want to do to her. He only wants to use her to control you. And so you know, he thinks that's going to be an easy feat. He doesn't have the slightest idea that we're not human, even though he's had firsthand knowledge of us nearly slapped in his face. He still is convinced that there are no such things as paranormals."

"I don't understand why that would be important to him. Why would he even care at this point? I don't know what to make of him or this." Gerard told her even if she were to give him what he wanted, he was still going to kill her. "But why? I don't love him. I never did. He put a gun to my head and made me marry him. For what? Just so he could?"

"Pretty much." She knew that, of course, but it didn't make her feel any better to have it confirmed. "You want this to end or do you want him to be able to make your life a living hell for the rest of your life? It's pretty simple really. He ends. I don't mean to tell you that we'll kill him. But if it comes to it, we will. But wouldn't you like to be able to take a deep breath, have a nice relaxing afternoon making love to Darin all day?"

"Yes. But I don't want anyone to be responsible for his death. I don't want to have to think that you murdered someone for me." Gerard handed her a picture, and she looked at it. Her hands were shaking when she handed it back to him. "You want to do this to him? How is that any better than a pack of cougars killing him?"

"That's Mr. Donaldson. An eighty-four-year-old man that did nothing more than own a house that Crosby wanted. The poor old man had buried his wife a few years ago. She was buried nearby his home so that he could walk to her grave every day and lay flowers on it. And according to his neighbors, he did just that. While he was out one day, just a few feet from his back door, Crosby came into his home, took it over, and did that to him when he came inside." The man had been mutilated, his body beaten. His throat had been cut, and it looked like his legs and arms had been broken as well. "What do you suppose he'll do to your daughter when he gets her? Do you think he'll be gentle with her?"

"No." Gerard said that he didn't think so either. "And so you know, I don't care for this scare tactic either. You could have told me that he only beat the man to death."

Gerard said nothing but sat there. Darin took the picture and looked at it before handing it back to his brother. Mercedes and Gerard stared at each other until she had to look away. The man was scarier than the rest of his family. She had a feeling that Gerard could and would do anything to keep them all safe.

In the end they agreed to disagree on the way that Nash was out of their lives. As she took the banking information from Emma, all she could think about was they were willing to kill for her. And had. Bonnie had been hurt and they had taken care of the man responsible without a backward glance. Mercedes could almost feel sorry for Nash. Almost, but she knew that what happened to him was going to depend on what he did or said when they took him.

~~~

Nash tried to think where he could lay his hands on some money as he made a few calls. Now…he needed as much as he could lay his hands on right this very minute. It didn't help matters that his accounts were empty. The two credit cards that he'd stolen a few months ago were cancelled. The one he had in a fake name had been cut up by the store manager when he'd gone to get himself a new suit, something that he did when he was upset or down in the dumps. And now that had been taken from him as well. The phone in his hand rang and rang, and he was getting worried that something really had happened to Rocky.

There was no way that these people had killed him. They weren't the killing type. They were more of the call in the cops and have them deal with it sort of people. He was the killer, not them. But the longer he tried to call his friend, the more and more he was afraid that he'd underestimated them. And in the end, Nash was going to make them pay for that as well.

Almost as soon as he ended the call, it rang again and he was relieved to see his attorney's name on the screen. He would do what he needed. It's what he paid him for. But before he could get too far into the mental list Nash had, he cut him off.

"I'm sorry, but I can't help you. I suppose I could, but I'm not going to. You're on your own, Mr. Crosby." Nash asked him what he was talking about. "We were notified this morning that you were being pursued in the death of four people. Not to mention you've left the state. How many times were you warned that you couldn't do that unless you notified someone? There are others charges too. A gun that has your fingerprints on it. Stolen property—"

"I have personal business with my wife. She left me no choice but to go after her and bring her to heel. Now as I was saying, I need for you to—" The man corrected him that it was his ex-wife. "So everyone keeps telling me. I never got to have my say in the story that she spun for the judge. So as far as I'm concerned, she's still mine. She did this behind my back and I'll not have it."

"You sound like a spoiled child. You'll not have it? She's yours? You're wrong on both counts by the way. And she only needed to show up and let them see the police reports, the hospital records. As well as bring in testimony from the few people that she could get to write her something that stated what sort of person you were. There were pictures too, I'm told. Of the violence you committed against her. I've told you, time and time again, she is off-limits to you. Move on." He told him he couldn't, not without her where she should have been all along. "Then you're going to lose this war you're taking out against her. I'm just glad that I won't be a part of it."

"You'll do as I tell you or so help me...." Nash let out a long breath and tried his best to get control of his temper. "I need you to look into my accounts. There is money missing. All of it, as a matter of fact. How is it that someone was able to get into my personal accounts and take my money like that? Not to mention, the house that is mine is now in Mer's name. I want that looked into as well."

"I would imagine the same way that you got someone to take *her* money from *her* accounts. You stole it. But I don't really care. As I said, I no longer work for you. Why I even started working for you in the first place is still a mystery to me. I did you a favor and you fucked me over. I'm done."

When the line went dead, Nash hit redial. There was no way that this little shit was going to end this relationship because he said so. But when the call went straight to voice mail, he decided that he was going to take care of him as soon as he got back to his home. If he could ever get back there.

After the visit yesterday from the supposed vampire and the animals with that Douglas person, he'd done a lot of thinking. The vampire had been wearing fake teeth. The animals were well trained movie set animals. He was still trying to work out the one where Darin had turned into the cougar, but he would. There were no such things as shifters and vampires, and anyone that believed that shit should be shot in the head and put out of his misery. If there were, he was sure he would have read about it somewhere. Or he would have seen a couple of them. People were ready to believe everything that came along. Nash was not.

The doorbell rang as he was making his way to the kitchen for some much needed coffee. There wasn't anyone to make it for him now. Rocky had taken care of that. But he still needed the caffeine hit. His nerves were fried.

Nash approached the door quietly. He didn't just open the door anymore. He watched and waited, trying to see what the person on the other side of door was about. When the man simply put a box on the stoop, Nash waited until he was gone before he went out and picked it up. But the man coming out of the shadows made him scream a little. Nash was going to kill the fucker. However, the gun at his head had him standing perfectly still.

"You're going to come along with me." Nash tried to turn his head but was prevented from that when the guy knocked the gun against his head. "I said that you're coming with me, not that you were going to do some sightseeing while you were at it."

"What's this about? I've done nothing wrong." The man laughed. "At least tell me who you are. So when I'm finished here, I can hunt you down and kill your motherfucking ass."

He was shoved into the back of a van, and the doors slammed shut before he could try to get a good look at the stranger who'd put him in here. Another guy sat in the passenger seat. There was a man in the back of the van with him, one that he was pretty sure he'd never seen before, but he had on a hoodie and Nash couldn't see his face. But no matter how many times Nash tried to get him to tell him what was going on, he did nothing but sit there like he'd done this a thousand times. Nash wanted to knock the shit out of the man but was sort of afraid of him. He had seen some pretty crazy shit over the last few days. Then the driver got in and he was knocked around again.

Yesterday when he'd gone out to get the paper, he'd seen a man that looked like Rocky. Nash had yelled for him to come to him, and the man had rushed him, knocking Nash on his ass and busting his head on the pavement. When he woke, only a few minutes had passed he was sure, but his clothing was all mussed up. His tie was undone and his shoes were scuffed. Going into the house, he looked himself over in the mirror to find that he'd been wounded too.

Cuts under his arms had startled him. There was a bite mark on his throat. In addition to his shoes looking like he'd walked a few hundred miles in them, his socks were missing, the zipper in his pants broken. The harder he tried to remember what had happened, the fuzzier things got. Like he could no longer remember what he'd gone outside for. What he had for lunch or breakfast. It was as if his mind had been messed with.

Later that day, after taking a long hot shower, he'd gone to where he'd hung all his suits. That's when he noticed that all the shirts he'd brought with him were stained. There was blood, a rusty color, on each of them in different spots on his clothing. Some more than others, but blood all the same.

His pants had been knotted at the legs. It had taken him twenty minutes to find a pair that didn't look too bad so he could wear them. All his shoes had been soiled. Some of them looked as if someone had filled them with shit. He'd been so nervous all afternoon that he'd not left the living room except to go to the bathroom. And even then he'd checked under the sink and in the small linen closet before using the commode. Today wasn't much different in the weird shit going on either.

When the van stopped, he was tossed around again. The man sitting in the back with him didn't even move, not even when the van lurched forward again. As soon as the doors were opened again he tried to get away, but the two men from the front seats dragged him out by his feet. His head hit the bumper twice, then the ground. Someone was going to pay for this. He was going to make sure of it.

Sitting up, he got to look around. They were in the middle of the woods. There didn't appear to be a telephone, much less a house, around for miles. Even the trees looked like someone hadn't touched them in decades, the poison ivy growing up them as thick as his arm.

"What the fuck is the meaning of this?" If Nash was honest with himself, which he rarely was, he would admit that he was terrified. These men were going to hurt him, and badly. "Take me back right now."

"This is the way this is going to work. And so you know, I'd rather just kill your fucking ass, but I made a promise to someone and I have to keep it." He wondered aloud where this person was. "Safe. At home, I guess, with the family. You're going to answer a few questions for us and you're going to tell us the truth. Then when we've gotten what we want, you're going to go to away for a very long time."

"You think so? Well, I have news for you. That is not going to happen. I don't care what sort of deal you made with Mer or whoever you made a promise to. You tell her that she's next on my shit list." He found himself lifted up off the ground and pinned against the side of the van. The man that had spoken was holding him there with nothing more than his hand, and that made him think of the man who had claimed he was a vampire.

"Did you kill Alfred Donaldson?" He wanted to lie to him, tell him to fuck off at the very least, but he couldn't. Not with the hand around his throat. And it felt like he was choking on the words when they tried to get past his lips. Nash shook his head and felt it bang against the metal at his head. "Do you know who killed Donaldson? And what was done to him?"

"Rocky did. He loves to play when he murders. Sometimes he can get out of hand, but I don't care so long as the results are the same." The thoughts of lying to this man evaporated with each question. The man asked him what happened to the body. "I don't know what he did to him, but he was gone and that's all I cared about."

"Were you aware that you broke the law to come here? That as a condition of your release that you were to report to your parole officers weekly and not leave the state?" Nash nodded. "Say it, damn it. We need to have you say it."

"Yes. But who gives a shit? They rarely know who you are when you call in. And I had business to take care of that didn't leave me any choice but to leave the state. This is all my wife's fault. Well, my ex-wife's fault. She left when I didn't tell her she could." He tried to clamp his mouth closed, but the man asked him if he understood that once you divorced someone, that ended things. "No. I don't care what sort of paper she had filed. She's mine until I kill her."

"You plan to kill her? You want to kill Mercedes?" He felt his nose running then, the blood running down over his lips and to his chin. "Answer me."

"Yes, I'm going to fucking kill her. And that fucking brat she birthed too. Things might have been different had she given me a son, but she didn't. Not that I think that one is mine. Have you seen her? She looks like she could be anyone's kid." The man let him go. Nash had fallen to the ground, but he wasn't hurt. They would be, but for now he would let them think they'd won. "So we're done here? You got what you wanted?"

"No, I got enough, but not what I wanted." That made no sense to him, but before he could ask him what the fuck that meant, one of the other men stood in front of him.

"Mr. Nash Crosby, you're here to pay for the murder of Alfred Donaldson, Rocky Bends, Millie Sanders, Allen Jack—"

"I didn't kill Rocky. He was my friend." The man looked over at the first one. "This guy, Douglas someone, came by and gave me body parts of him. But I never killed him. Look at him for that." Neither man spoke, and for some reason Nash felt the need to fill in the quiet. "Rocky was my friend. I'd never kill him. He knew too much about me to let go, but I'd never kill him. As for those other people, you can blame that on Mer too. Had she just done what she was told, none of this would have had to happen."

"Be that as it may, you still were responsible for a lot of people dying, Crosby. And we're here to make sure that you pay for each one of them." He looked around, then back at the man. The gun in his hand was dangerously close, but Nash wasn't worried. If they had wanted him dead, he'd be there.

"You won't kill me that way. It would be cold blooded murder, and I know enough about your kind to know that cops, for the most part, follow a set of rules. And murder isn't on that list." Nash laughed when he put the gun to his head. "One thing I've learned over the years is to spot a man who is good at doing the right thing. That would be you. You can no more pull that trigger than I can turn straight. You just don't have it in you."

The man backed off, and Nash stood there. He wasn't worried now. They didn't have it in them to kill him. But they would knock him around a bit. That might be painful for a while, but he'd live to hunt them down and make sure they never bothered him again. These men were going to die, of course, but not today. He realized that the two of them were talking and moved closer to listen.

"I knew this wasn't going to work. I said that when we got called in to do this. The man is a real bastard and he thinks he's right." The second man only nodded, and he had a feeling they were talking about Mer. "No one is going to be happy when we go back. I'm not, so I'm sure that other people aren't going to be either."

"You should have brought her with you. I'd really like to tell her what I think of her. Damned bitch owes me a great deal of money. And if she thinks I'm going to just let her get away with this shit because you two were too stupid to pull the trigger, then she's gonna learn not to trust me." He laughed and the two men looked at him with a confused look on their faces. Or stupid, Nash wasn't sure. "Not that she ever did trust me. Not even when I took her out the first time. Well, took her out wasn't right. I took her."

"Somebody said you forced her into marrying you. That you held a gun to her head to make her do it and threatened the life of her father." Nash nodded. He was feeling pretty good now and didn't care if these idiots knew what he'd done. He was going to walk, plain and simple. "You're a sick fuck, you know that?"

"Yeah, but I'm a man that gets what he wants when he wants it. She might have been better off if she'd just given me what I wanted. I don't like to be thwarted when I have a plan in mind. Nor do I like it when I can't have something I want. And I wanted her. The only reason I married her was because she was so high and mighty about things. The stupid cunt should have died right away, but I wanted to play. Then she got knocked up. Mother fuck. No matter what I tried to do, that kid would not go away. Not even when I shoved her mother down the stairs a few times. Hung on like they meant business."

Nash was saying too much. He knew this. It was like in all those dump programs on television that Rocky used to watch. They'd wrap it all up with the bad guy pretty much confessing everything he'd done and why. These two were about the stupidest cops he'd ever encountered. As he made his way around the van to see if they had left the keys in it, he thought of all the things he was going to do to Mer when he got her back. Things might be delayed a bit, but she was going to get it but good.

No keys. When he made his way back to where he'd been sitting, the two men were gone, but the one from the back of the van was standing there. He'd forgotten about him and wondered why he'd not been pulled out of the van when he had.

Nash backed up. He'd not realized how fucking huge the man was when they'd been in the van together. He asked him where the idiots had gone.

"They're busy." He pulled the hoodie off his face. He looked like a kid, his face almost smooth like a young boy's.

180

Nash wondered if he was even old enough to drive yet. "I'm much older than you think. And the other two, they never said they were cops, now did they? They work for me."

The man nodded, and Nash turned to look in the direction he did. The two men were digging a hole, and Nash turned to look at the younger man.

"What are they doing?" He smiled, his mouth full of long sharp teeth. "What are you? What are you going to do?"

"Digging your grave. Your worst nightmare, and I'm going to kill you." Nash took two steps and felt the pain down his back. As he was being dragged backward, he screamed for help. The other two men only continued to dig his grave. Nash realized he was a dead man.

CHAPTER 13

Darin closed the door and turned and looked at Mercedes. The police had come by to tell them that Nash was gone. Just gone. His clothing and other things were still in the house. The police said he'd gone out earlier to get the paper and he'd gone back in the house, but they hadn't seen him since. That when they'd gone there to arrest him, he simply wasn't there.

"Did you do this? Or any of your brothers?" He shook his head at Mercedes's question. "You won't lie to me, right? You didn't have him killed?"

"No. You made us promise to do this the legal way and we were going to. I swear to you, I had nothing to do with his disappearance. And while the police were here, I asked Mason and the others and they didn't either." She stood there. Shell shocked was all he could think about. "Maybe he gave up."

"You know as well as I do that he wasn't going to ever give up." Darin nodded but watched her. He wasn't sure what she was so upset about. He was gone, shouldn't that make her happy? "What if he's out there, just waiting for us to get relaxed enough that he can attack and kill me?"

"Do you really think that?" She shook her head. "Neither do I. I think he's dead somewhere. I don't know who might have done this, but I'm betting that someone has killed him." He moved across the hallway to take her into his arms.

"I'm afraid, Darin. I feel like everything is perfect right now, and something is going to happen to take it all away. I wish now I would have let you do it your way. At least then I would know for sure."

Darin did as well but didn't say anything. She was upset enough as it was. Holding her in his arms, he thought of tomorrow and what he'd planned for her and Bonnie. He thought now would be a great time to give it to her.

"Your birthday is tomorrow." She looked up at him, frowning, and asked him who had told him. "Okay, so I had no idea when it was until Bonnie mentioned it. But I got you something."

As he reached for his jacket and the envelope, he felt the little box in his pocket that was also part of her birthday. He was going to give that to her when they were having dinner tomorrow night.

She took the envelope and opened it. When she read each of the tickets, including the ones to the opera house in town, he watched her face light up. He felt pretty good about what he'd done, and then she started crying. Now he wasn't so sure. Darin had wanted her to like this so badly, and he told her he was sorry.

"I thought you'd like a little pampering after all this stress. And then Holly suggested the opera. I actually don't know that I've been to the one in town, but thought it would be fun. Then there is the dinner. I know the chef is really good and that he can—"

She put her hand over his mouth, and he licked it. "You're the sweetest man I know." Darin nodded and laughed when she smacked him on the shoulder. "I've never been to an opera either. And to have a spa day with my favorite people? This is so wonderful. I can't believe that you thought of it. Not that you're not smart, but it is a sort of girly thing and that —"

He didn't shut her up with his hand but with his mouth. And when she melted against him, all he could think about was being inside of her. His cat moved along his skin as if to say that he wanted her too. Darin pressed her against the wall and backed away from her.

"Take it all off." She pulled her shirt up and over her head. He did the same. "When you're naked I'm going to let my cat have his fill. Then I'm going to eat you. After you come so many times that you can't stand up, I'm going to fuck you hard enough to make walking difficult."

"Yes, please." Darin was naked before she was and let his cat take him. When she took her panties off, his cat moved in and licked her pussy while she held on to his fur. Darin wasn't sure he'd ever get enough of her and wondered if his cat would either. Having her to feast on was one of the greatest pleasures he'd ever had.

When his cat backed off, Darin took his body and buried his mouth over her dripping pussy and fucked her with his fingers. The more he drank of her the more he needed. Even when she begged him to stop, that she could no longer stand on her own, he ate her. Sucking on her clit and fucking her hard with his tongue was giving him everything he needed. When she jerked his head up, he looked up at her

"Fuck me. Now." He stood up, his cock so hard it hurt when she wrapped her fingers around him. "Fuck me, Darin. I want to feel you hard inside of me."

Turning her so that she faced the wall, he told her to hold onto the table there. When she bent at the waist, he walked up behind her and slammed his cock deep. He was too close for foreplay, not that she needed it. She was soaking wet and tight for him. Darin wanted it to last, to make her come several times before he took his own pleasure, but she'd teased him all morning before the police had shown up. Now he had to have all of her.

Holding her to him, he leaned over her and took her as hard as he could. When she slid her fingers into her pussy and touched him, Darin saw stars. His cock actually felt like she'd shocked him with something electrical.

Christ, she was going to make him come too soon. Fucking her harder, trying to think of anything but coming, she told him to bite her. His cat snarled at him to do it, and he snapped his mouth around her shoulder and tore into her flesh.

Her screams of pleasure brought him over the edge. Coming this way, buried deep inside of her, had him coming again, twice more before he felt that he could no longer move. And when she slumped over the table, he picked her up and held her to him.

He'd hurt her when he'd bitten her. He knew that, and he felt just horrible for it. When her shaking made him ache more, he lifted her chin up to see that she wasn't crying but laughing. He asked her what was so funny.

"You are. You can be the most gentle and loving man one minute and this savage the next. I love it, the way you can just be so animal-like and loving at the same time." Darin kissed her nose. "And you make me feel like I could take on the world and win."

"I want you to win." He put her down and the two of them dressed. The police coming by had interrupted their morning, and they both needed to get back on track. Each of them had a great deal to do, and the sooner they got it done, the sooner they could get back here to their home.

Mason was in his front yard when Darin came out of the house a few minutes after Mercedes left on foot to go to the clinic.

"Is there a reason that your wife isn't driving the car we gave her?" Darin told him the reason she gave him. "I see. It's her car to get back and forth with. We wanted her to use it all the time."

"Then I'd like to suggest you tell her that." Mason said that he would. "What are you really doing here? You could have asked her when she got to work this morning."

"Zach." Darin nodded and went to his beat up truck. "Were you going to tell me about it or was I going to be the last to know?"

"Again, you could have asked him. If you're pissy about it, I would like to suggest that you cool off before talking to him. He's pretty proud of himself. And I think that if you were to piss him off, Mercedes might make you regret it. So would Landon." Darin tossed his hat on the seat and turned the key to his truck. He wasn't surprised that it didn't start. The stupid thing was as old as he was. But he was in too good of a mood to let it fuck up his day. "Can you give me a lift to work? I'm late now."

"I can't. But I can give you a truck." Darin shook his head. "Sorry, little brother, it's the new family policy that Jace and our wives have come up with. That we all have reliable cars, as well as safe housing. Most of us have that, but we—you and I—are going to go over and convince Zach that we are going to help him out too."

"I don't want you to buy me a car." Mason said it was too bad, it was done. "What the fuck is wrong with this one?"

"Well, it won't start most mornings when the weather isn't near perfect. The tires are as bald as Mr. Sloan's head from high school shop class. The battery is seven years past its expiration date, and it's needed a new engine since the day you bought it for too much off of Peter Luster when you turned sixteen. Take the damned car we got for you." He looked to where Mason pointed. "It's four wheel drive too. No more worrying about your ass sliding all over the road when you have to go out in the snow with my niece."

Picking up his hat, Darin put it on and walked to the big blue truck. Christ, it was pretty. Four doors, hard-covered bed, and a snow plow on the front of it. As he ran his fingers down the side of it, all he could think about was riding around in something that was younger than his daughter. Looking at Mason, he asked him why he'd done it.

"We did talk, Jace and I. We have it better than most. A love that won't ever grow old, enough money that we never have to work if we don't want to. And family. One we should have been taking care of." He told him about the money from Nash. "I knew about that. But that doesn't negate the fact that we should have done more for you and the others. A safe truck is a small thing when I think of all the things you've done for us. For all of us."

"I didn't do anything that any other family wouldn't have done." Mason didn't even bother saying anything. Over the last several months, they had learned the hard way that families like theirs were the oddity, not the norm. "Is this your way of buttering me up to talk to Zach? I have to tell you, he's pretty set on making this work by himself."

"I know that. What I want you to do for me is act as my representative when it comes to his fields. Jace and I want to buy into his first three years of crops so that he can get a start. We figured that if he even charged us ten percent off what we pay now, we'd save about three million over those first years." Darin said he'd done the math too, and it was more like six million. "He means to plant it all then."

"Yes. And he was going to go to you about three fields that you have empty right now. He figures you'd cut him a good deal on them for a lower price on the grain." Mason got in the new truck. "We going somewhere? I have to get to work."

"Jessie said he'd cover for you. Julia—good choice, by the way, on hiring her—has breakfast going, and said that when you do get there, she wanted you to set her up so she can do her own ordering for the kitchen." Mason grinned at him. "See, I can be helpful too."

The truck started on the first turn of the key. Darin looked at his big brother and told him he loved him. "I don't think I say that enough to any of you. And I do, love you I mean."

"I love you too, but let's get going. You might have the morning off, but I have shit to get done. And my wife is up for election this year. I expect your votes." Darin nodded. "Oh, and something else. I wanted to talk to you about expanding the Douglas House."

~~~

"Thank you for this." Austin only nodded and took the small envelope. "If you ever need a favor, you know that I'll do it for you."

"You know that I'll never be able to repay you for what you've done for me." Paddy said nothing. As far as he was concerned, that debt had been paid long ago. "He was a monster. More than that, he was one that did not care what he did so long as he would benefit from it."

"He hurt my future daughter-in-law. For that alone he needed to die." Paddy watched Austin sit down. There was little about the man across from him that made him think of calm seas. More like a turbulent storm where people died. "Will anyone ever find him? I mean, his body?"

"Never. I made sure that he will be fodder before the next season of planting. And you have ensured that no one will use that land again. Not so long as I live." The envelope disappeared in Austin's jacket pocket. The deed inside of it gave Austin four acres, all he'd wanted to take out the man that would have haunted them all for a very long time. "You never said he was her father, this child that will mate with your son. Do you think she'll be upset should she find out?"

"Will she find out?" Austin laughed and said she'd not hear it from him. "Then I don't have to think about it. But I'd say that if she's anything like her mother, who I've discovered she is a great deal like, then yes, she would be. But you know as well as I do that he would never have stopped."

"No, he was a man set in his ways. They would eventually lead him down a path that would kill him, but there is no telling how much he might have done before that." Paddy nodded. "You're a good man, Paddy Sexton. Why have I not noticed that before now?"

"You were too busy being a hit man for some very unsavory people." Austin said there was that. "And hiding out. Do you suppose they still hunt for you?"

"No. I think they believe me dead, just as you said that they would." Paddy had made sure the right people had seen the man's body before he'd converted him. "You saved not just my life but my future. I know you think us even, but we will never be so far as I'm concerned. I wish I could do more for you."

"You've done more than a friend should have." Austin said nothing. "Someday I'd like for you to meet the Douglas men and women. They're a group of people that I think you'd enjoy. Smart, savvy, and on top of things. Nothing like the previous owners of the land were. Except for McBride. There is a man of men."

"Him I have met. And his son. I heard that he was dead." Paddy said that he was. "Good. There was a monster I would gladly have taken care of, too, if things fell my way."

"When are you leaving? Or do you want to stay around for a while? I'd like that. It's been a long time since I've had someone to talk to." Austin stood up and put out his hand, and Paddy took it in his as he spoke. "Yeah, I didn't think you'd want to hang around."

"It's been good to see you again, my friend. I have sorely missed you." Paddy said the same for him. "When I return, and I will, I should like to meet these Douglas men. They sound like people that would help an old wolf like me find peace."

"They will at that. Things are moving along for them now. I'm looking into a few things for them...they're good men to work with." Austin nodded and moved to the door. "Thank you again for taking care of this for my family."

"It was my pleasure. As I said, he was a monster and you did well to have him removed." Paddy hugged Austin, and then he faded into the night without a sound. Paddy wondered if he were to go out there now if he'd walk right by the man without ever knowing it. Instead of going into the house, Paddy sat on the swing and watched the stars come out.

"Dad?" Paddy looked up at his son when he came outside. "I thought I heard you talking to someone. Are you okay?"

"Yes, as fine as rain. How are you? You and Bonnie get all your homework done?" Patrick hadn't been a very good student until recently. Paddy would bet his last dollar that the pretty little wolf on the ranch had something to do with that.

"She helped me with my math. She scolded me for not paying attention in class." His son leaned his head back on the swing. Paddy wondered why when he'd said that to him, it hadn't mattered as much as it did when Bonnie had said it to him. "I have to start taking notes too. She said that she'd help me put them in order so that I can study better."

Paddy found himself smiling in the dark. Christ almighty, she was going to make his son into something. But he didn't comment on her methods or her rules about notes and such. He wanted his son to feel secure in coming to talk to him, and making fun of him wouldn't make that last very long.

They talked for over an hour. Not about anything in particular, but they did touch on a lot of things. The upcoming fishing trip the two of them were going on. Julia's job. And how happy his mom seemed to be all the time now.

"Do you think that Bonnie will want to have a job too?" Paddy wasn't sure how to answer that, but before he could clarify a few things first, Patrick spoke again. "I'd like to be able to support her so that she can just be a stay-at-home mom like Mom used to be. But I see Mom and how happy she is, and I wonder if Bonnie would be too. And the money coming in would be good too. I know I have a while, but I was looking at houses, and they're really expensive."

"You have to feed the two of you too. And there are other things like phone, electric, and gas. It's expensive being out on your own." Patrick said he'd seen that. "You let her do what she wants and I think you'll make her happy. I heard her telling your mom that she wanted to be a doctor. A human doctor. That'll be expensive to study too, but I think she'd be good at it."

"I think she'd be good at whatever she wanted to be." Paddy thought that was a good answer. "Well, Dad, I'm going off to bed. Bonnie is going to do this girl thing with her mom and aunt's tomorrow, so I was wondering if you wanted to go hunting, just the two of us. It might be fun since Mom is working anyway."

"I'd love that, son. I surely would." Paddy sat there for an hour longer than he should have, just thinking about life in general.

Thanks to the Douglases, there were jobs now. Money coming into the coffers. People were coming back to pack life again, and he had a good family. Paddy stood up and looked out over the woods that he and the pack had claimed. Yes, sir, he thought, he had a good life here now.

Now Available in the
Pride of the Double Deuce Series

Jace
Pride of the Double Deuce
Book 1

Mason
Pride of the Double Deuce
Book 2

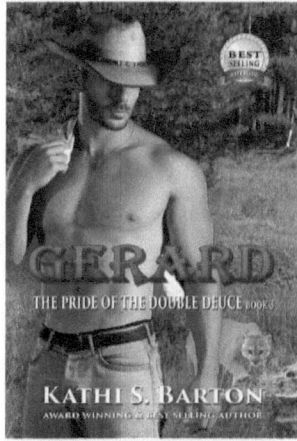

Gerard
Pride of the Double Deuce
Book 3

Darin
Pride of the Double Deuce
Book 4

.

Before You Go...

HELP AN AUTHOR

write a review

THANK YOU!

Share your voice and help guide other readers to these wonderful books. Even if it's only a line or two your reviews help readers discover the author's books so they can continue creating stories that you'll love. Login to your favorite retailer and leave a review. Thank you.

AWARD WINNING, BESTSELLING AUTHOR

Kathi Barton, winner of the Pinnacle Book Achievement award as well as a best-selling author on Amazon and All Romance books, lives in Nashport, Ohio with her husband Paul. When not creating new worlds and romance, Kathi and her husband enjoy camping and going to auctions. She can also be seen at county fairs with her husband who is an artist and potter.

Her muse, a cross between Jimmy Stewart and Hugh Jackman, brings her stories to life for her readers in a way that has them coming back time and again for more. Her favorite genre is paranormal romance with a great deal of spice. You can visit Kathi on line and drop her an email if you'd like. She loves hearing from her fans. aaronskiss@gmail.com.

Follow Kathi on her blog:
http://kathisbartonauthor.blogspot.com/